THREE STORIES

THREE STORIES

Edited & Introduced by

TAHIR SHAH

The Scheherazade Foundation

The Scheherazade Foundation CIC
85 Great Portland Street
London
W1W 7LT
United Kingdom
www.SF.Charity
info@SF.Charity

First published by The Scheherazade Foundation CIC, 2023

THREE STORIES

The Purple Sapphire & Other Posthumous Papers
Christopher Blayre (Pseudonym of Edward Heron-Allen)
Philip, Allan & Co.
1921

The $30,000 Bequest & Other Stories
Mark Twain
Harper & Bros.
1906

The Parasite
Sir Arthur Conan Doyle
Constable & Co.
1894

ISBN 978-1-915311-25-2

CONTENTS

Series Introduction

From EARLIEST CHILDHOOD, I was told stories.

Of course, I was – most children are told stories.

After all, telling children stories is one of the foundations that makes their early experiences a childhood.

But as I think back to the first years of my own life, I find myself reeling from the sheer quantity of stories my infant ears took in.

Whereas other children my age were told stories for amusement, my parents (and the people they associated with) recounted the endless streams of tales for a different reason.

In their opinion, stories – and the ability to tell them – were part of an ancient alchemy... a way of processing complex ideas, of solving problems, and of developing the human mind.

My father, the writer and thinker Idries Shah, believed that folklore was the single most important breakthrough ever developed by the human species. The way he saw it, the rise of stories was as consequential as the development of the languages in which they were told.

He would say that, without stories and storytelling, humanity would never have evolved in the way that it has – and that the folktales, which form a bedrock of ancient societies, are more precious than any physical artefact unearthed on an archaeological dig.

As the years of my own childhood slipped by, I found myself unbothered to work out the hidden layers within treasuries of stories – what my father called 'instruction manuals to the world'. Like everyone else, I simply absorbed the individual tales, delighting in them.

And that's it – the key point, the genius of stories and storytelling.

It's a thing I only grasped in adulthood… something that fascinates me deeply.

In the same way you can jump into a car and drive across the country without giving a second thought to the engine or how it works, you can appreciate stories without understanding the hidden layers and devices that make them what they are.

Stories are all around us.

They're in the TV and movies we so adore, in the video games we play, and of course in the books we read. They're in newspapers and magazines, too; in the conversations we share with old friends, and with new ones. They're on our mobile phones, in aeroplanes, in submarines, and even in our dreams.

Our obsession with, and craving for, stories rests squarely with the way we are so absorbed by them, just as it does with the way we don't need to continually consider how and why they work.

Throughout my life, I've devoted an increasing amount of time to gathering stories from all corners of the world.

It began in my late teens, when I began to criss-cross the continents in a crazed preoccupation with folklore. I developed a first-hand love affair with societies that, over millennia, gave birth to their own astonishing traditions of stories and storytelling.

Most of the time, when reading or listening to stories, we forget that these tales have been shaped through the passage of time. Like pebbles in a river smoothed by rushing waters, they were honed through centuries of telling and retelling.

When I was twelve years old, my father published a masterwork, *World Tales*. The first edition was very large and featured hundreds of original illustrations. The book was unlike any that had come before, for it detailed the provenance and history of each story told.

At bedtime one night, he presented me with an advanced copy. For as long as I could remember, my father had been talking about the project.

Having an actual copy in my hands at last was thrilling beyond words.

Peering down at me sternly, my father said:

'This is far more than a book, Tahir Jan. It's the foundation stone of a great building... a building that *is* human culture. As you grow older, and as you go out into the world, you will understand that the folklores contained between the covers of *World Tales* have brought amusement and educated, and have solved problems when they were needed most of all.'

My father was right.

When I eventually headed out into the wilds of the world for the first time, I discovered the stories contained in *World Tales* for myself, along with a great many more. Just as he said, the stories published in his treasury were the warp and weft threads of society. Stories are the matrix on which culture itself is based – a framework that enables daily life to continue as smoothly as it does.

In this series of books, we have drawn together stories from all over the world. It's a mission begun decades ago by *World Tales*.

Some of the pieces will be known to you, and others will not.

Some will be easy to comprehend, while others will be challenging, or even nonsensical.

I'd now like to note something else…

The Occidental world seems to assume stories must appear in certain regimented ways – presented with a well-defined beginning, a middle, and an end. You know what I mean: the protagonist winning against all odds, and the happy ending to it all.

In the ancient tradition of teaching stories, the kind recounted for an eternity around campfires in the desert and in longhouses deep in the jungle, there's no such standardisation.

Rather, there's usually a hotchpotch of conflicting threads: stories without a straight linear narrative but with an underlying turbulence that gets the reader, or the listener, to sit up and think.

at The Scheherazade Foundation, we are preoccupied with the way we can extract knowledge from stories – either deliberately, or in a less structured way.

We hold the firm opinion that, in order to remove the marrow from the bone stories are best served up in the way as they were passed from one generation to the next throughout human history.

In this series, we have drawn together tales that were gathered in particular during the nineteenth and early twentieth centuries. Spanning a vast range of cultures, they offer an extraordinary glimpse into the societies from which they are drawn – societies that were often changed shortly afterwards by social upheaval, technologies, and war.

Indeed, the fact any of them were recorded at all is a thing of wonder.

Intriguingly, some of the tales will now appear dated because vocabulary and writing styles have altered. But the fact that they seem old-fashioned is of great interest – proof of the way stories are constantly changing and evolving from one era to the next.

Over the last thirty years, I've gathered hundreds of tales on my own journeys, most of them spoken directly into my ears by storytellers and fellow travellers, by wizened old men in the middle of nowhere, and by anyone else good enough to indulge my pleas.

On all those zigzagging adventures, one story sticks out, tantalising me whenever I turn it around my head.

It was called 'The Man Who Turned into a Cat'.

The reason I mention it here is not because it was an especially fine tale, but rather because, from that moment, it affected the way I perceive the world.

It was as though I were a lock and that, by hearing the tale, a key had been slipped into me and turned.

Since first receiving it, I've never been quite the same, my state of consciousness having been flipped inside out.

The fellow traveller who recounted 'The Man Who Turned into a Cat' was lost in shadow, no more than a fragment of his left cheek protruding shyly into the light.

We were sitting on low divans in a teahouse in the ancient Afghan city of Herat.

When the tale had been whispered, I sat there in silence for a long while.

'What have you done to me?' I asked after a long pause.

The fellow traveller offered half a smile.

'*I* didn't do anything,' he replied. 'It's the story that's affected you – a story that I myself first heard when I was a child playing in the orchards of Balkh.'

Peering into the shadow, my eyes widened.

'I don't understand,' I said feebly. 'After all, it's not an especially grand story. There wasn't even a jinn.'

The traveller's mouth eased out from the shadows.

Very slowly, it grinned.

'Tales containing the greatest sustenance for a soul speak in the softest voice,' he said.

Tahir Shah

The Purple Sapphire

ON THE 24TH of June, 1920, a few months after my appointment to the Professorship of Mineralogy in the University of Cosmopoli, I received, as a gift to the Museum from the surviving executor of the late Sir Clement Arkwright, under the most dramatic conditions, the Purple Sapphire. The facts attendant upon its arrival were as follows:

Sir George Amboyne, the Regius Professor of Medicine came into my room and deposited upon my table a small package.

'This is for you,' he said, 'a gift to the Mineralogical Department, made under most unfortunate circumstances. An elderly man has been run over by a motor car just outside; he was brought in, very badly damaged, though not, I hope, fatally. As I was in the building I was sent for, and have done what I can pending his removal to Hospital. When he recovered consciousness, he said with some difficulty,

"The packet – where is the packet?"

'The porter, who had carried him in, produced this parcel, which the man had been carrying when he was run over. When he saw it, he said,

7

"For the Museum – Purple Sapphire – give it to them," then he lost consciousness again. You see it is addressed 'To the Mineralogist, University of Cosmopoli.' You had better take charge of it.'

'Rather an ill-omened way to receive a presentation, isn't it?' I observed.

'Very,' replied the Regius Professor.

'I suppose we had better open it?'

We did so. Beneath the outermost wrapper was an envelope, addressed 'To My EXECUTORS,' it was unsealed and contained a sheet of note paper upon which was written

'It is my earnest wish that this packet shall not be opened until twenty-five years after my death. When that time has elapsed, it is to be delivered to my eldest male direct heir. It contains the Purple Sapphire given to me by the younger son of Colonel George Cardew. Whether by that time its power of doing evil to its possessor will have waned or not, I cannot tell, but I earnestly recommend my heir to get rid of it, if he can, at the earliest possible opportunity. – Clement Arkwright, Bart.'

'This is very odd,' remarked Sir George; 'the poor old man downstairs was evidently on his way to deposit it, whatever it is, here. Let us have a look at it.'

The removal of the inner wrapper disclosed a sandalwood box. Inside that, closely fitting, was another; inside that, another. There were seven of them, one inside the other. In the last and smallest, wrapped in a piece of curious fine muslin was the Purple Sapphire.

It was without exception the finest stone I had ever seen, perfectly cut, of the most brilliant deep amethyst-purple, and the size of a flattened bantam's egg. It was set in a sort of cage; two silver snakes, with their tails in their mouths, ran round it above and below the circumferential edge, and these were connected and held together by twelve small silver 'plaques' inscribed with the twelve Signs of the Zodiac. On one side were two silver rings, evidently for suspension, and from these hung, so as to cover and conceal the stone, on one side a circular plaque, evidently of very ancient make, of the kind familiar to students of Occultism and of the rites of the so-called Rosicrucians as the Seal of the Tau – a Greek T, surrounded by a flat band on which were engraved the letters ABRACADABRA. This fell over the flat or 'table' side of the stone. Over the other, the faceted side, hung a pair of amethyst Scarabs, evidently early Egyptian, threaded upon, and held in place by, thick silver wire.

Whether it was the circumstances in which it had reached us, or for some other and inexplicable reason, as I held it in my hand I felt an overwhelming sensation of nausea and faintness. I handed it to the Regius Professor without a word. He turned it over in his hand, raised the Tau and the Scarabs, and then put it down on my table.

'What a beastly thing,' he observed. We looked at one another for a few moments in silence, but neither of us gave utterance to the thoughts that were in our minds. Probably we could not have done so if we had wanted to.

I was the first to break the silence – with an effort of which I felt ashamed.

'I think,' said I, 'we will take it straight up to the Museum.'

'Yes,' said Sir George, for God's sake let's get rid of it.' He was quite unconsciously reiterating the advice of Sir Clement Arkwright.

Using one of the lids as a tray, we carried the Purple Sapphire up to the Museum, and placed it in the table case by the door, destined to contain 'Recent Acquisitions' which had not yet been registered and classified.

When we came down again, the elderly gentleman had been removed to the nearest hospital, and his relations, as indicated by letters and cards in his pocket – his name was also Arkwright – had been notified by telephone.

That afternoon the Mineralogical wing of the University Museum was struck by lightning. The damage done was ghastly. Many priceless exhibits were destroyed, and several weeks elapsed before the room could be opened and used again.

The table case of 'Recent Acquisitions' was untouched.

***

It was perhaps a year after this that a card was brought to me bearing the name Sir Gilbert A. Arkwright.

I had not forgotten the Purple Sapphire, for the romance of its acquisition stuck to it, and students showed it to visitors as 'The Unlucky Stone,' and invented all kinds of fantastic stories about it.

The assistants and even the cleaner hated it.

One story went that it glowed at night with an unearthly refulgence – I was foolish enough to go up one winter evening when the lights were turned off to see for myself.

I saw nothing – but I confess to having experienced a sensation of – to put it mildly – extreme discomfort. I felt like a child afraid of the dark. Idiotic!

One of the cleaners declared that one evening when she was 'cleaning up,' a 'naked Heathen – and, what's worse, black,' had suddenly looked at her over the top of the case she was dusting, and that she would sooner lose her place than ever enter the Mineralogical wing again. Idiotic!

Well, – the card of Sir Gilbert Arkwright preceded the appearance of a charming young man of the regulation British athlete type, in the thirties I should say. In answer to my look of enquiry he said, easily:

'I think you have here a Purple Sapphire, which my uncle was bringing here the day he was killed in a street accident.'

I was shocked to hear this, and all the circumstances recurred at once to my mind. I murmured some conventional phrases, and the young man replied:

'Oh! That's all right. It was a terrible thing of course, but that was the last of it for us. We were none of us ever allowed to see it, but it was supposed to have been, and was called, 'the Curse of the Cardews' in my father and grandfather's time. I only came to bring you this book which turned up the other day in going over a lot of my poor old uncle's papers – we thought you might like to have it.'

He laid on my table a small quarto M.S. notebook of the cheap American-cloth covered type, the first page of which bore – without more – 'THE NAGPUR SAPPHIRE,' and the date, 1885. I was rather 'thrilled,' and having suitably thanked my visitor, he left me. That night I took the book home with me, and, after dinner, I sat down to read it.

There were only a few pages written upon – as is usual with notebooks – but the story they contained was so uncomfortably weird that I offer no apology for transcribing them in full. The original M.S. is in the library of the Mineralogical Department (M.M.3.b.36).

***

The M.S. of Sir Clement Arkwright

I hope and believe that I have made such arrangements and provisions as shall prevent any of my immediate descendants taking the Nagpur Sapphire into their custody, possession or control.

But as there exists a widely spread impression in my family that it is a jewel of great value and of exceptional beauty – which is indeed the case – I think that in the future some member of my family may be moved by curiosity or cupidity to claim possession of it. I will therefore write in this book my reasons for not wishing this to happen.

One of my earliest recollections is that of Colonel George Cardew and his wife. They lived in a poor little cottage – how poor I was then too young to appreciate – on the outskirts of the village nearest to my father's place in Shropshire. The Colonel used to give me pennies, and his wife cake, but the latter gifts were discounted by the fact that she was everlastingly advising my mother to give us castor oil, and periodically insisted upon our being taken to see the dentist.

We children resented this interference – if interference it really was – in the placid lives of an otherwise very happy family. The Colonel was an invalid and very lame, the result of a wound received in the Indian Mutiny, which continually gave him trouble; his wife was peevish, continually at war with Fate which held from her the position and wealth of a great lady.

In fact, as the saying goes, they had seen better times, and were ill-adapted to worse. They had two sons, Richard and George, who were the constant playfellows of my elder brothers. I was too young for them. These two boys, after they left Haileybury School, cut themselves adrift and set out to make their own way in the world by sheer grit and hard work.

Richard became a medical student, and as he was a sharp contrast to the lazy, rowdy class which constituted the medical students in those days – the early seventies – he passed his examinations with distinction, and, having no home prospects or capital, joined the Indian Army Medical Service – he was always known as 'Dr. Dick.' George won a Cadetship at Sandhurst, and, knowing that he had no one but himself to rely upon, worked hard, did well, and was in due course gazetted to an Indian Regiment, where he rose to be Major and was regarded as a very rising man –he was always known as 'Major George'.

Their sterling merits carried everything before them. In due course Dr. Dick left the Army Medical Service and became a successful physician in Simla. Major George, promoted to Colonel, became 'Resident' to one of the Indian Native rajahs, and was regarded as one of the really notable Administrators under the Indian Government. Their rare visits home were hailed with delight not only by their old parents but by all of us, for they brought home wonderful things from India as presents, and would talk –how they talked! Thrilling accounts of their lives out there, of dangers from rebels, from snakes, from wild beasts, from plagues –we were never tired of listening to them.

Then old Colonel Cardew died, and within a year his wife followed him to the grave. Though their later years were much ameliorated by handsome remittances from their sons, they were never happy. The Colonel was a terrible sufferer, and they were really unlucky, in small things as in great. If they saved money and invested it the investments went wrong – people always said that if they had wanted to cultivate weeds, or to encourage rats in their little place, the weeds would have refused to grow, or the rats to be encouraged. It was a sorry business when Dr. Dick came home to wind up his parents' affairs, and he returned to India a distressful man. He told us he was afraid to go back for he felt that his luck was gone. This was quite inexplicable to us, but lie was a true prophet, unfortunately.

An untoward 'accident' or two in his practice, one fatal one in the treatment of a great Maharajah, dragged him down from his professional eminence, a bank in which his savings were invested – an 'unlimited' concern – failed, and carried with it the whole of his savings, and in the end Dr. Dick, who was fortunately a bachelor, was reduced to living in a suburb of London on an allowance made him by Colonel George.

After some ten years of an aimless and unlucky existence he fell out of a railway train and was killed. There were those who did not hesitate to doubt whether his tragic death was accidental.

After his death Fate seemed to turn her malevolent attention to Colonel George. He became unpopular with succeeding Viceroys and lost influence and caste in the Service. Finally, not supported as he should have been by his Government, he came to loggerheads with his Maharajah; an insurrection in his native State was attributed to his management, or mismanagement. He was superseded and sent on a punitive expedition to the borders of Afghanistan.

In this affair he failed utterly and unaccountably. The natives, soldiers and civilians alike, seemed to hate him, and of the few faithful Sikhs whom he commanded only one returned with him. The rest had been killed –his other troops had practically deserted him. It was amazing, for until the death of Dr. Dick he was almost worshipped by the natives both civil and military.

On his return to Madras he twice escaped assassination by a miracle, and in the end he was 'retired' and came home to live on an inadequate pension, with his wife and two children. The change, I suppose it was, preyed upon his wife, and she went mad. His daughter died apparently of what was not then recognised as appendicitis, and his son, having gone utterly to the dogs, fortunately emigrated to New Zealand and was never heard of again.

It was then that I came into the story. Colonel George was, as I have indicated, some six or eight years my senior, but this did not count so much when I was thirty and living a rather luxurious bachelor life in London. Colonel George often came to my rooms and we used to talk over old times, and, on occasions, to dissipate mildly together. He was always cheerful, and seemed quite resigned to the ill luck that pursued him – he said that it did him good to be with me, for my 'good luck' was proverbial. I had health, wealth enough, and a reliance upon my lucky star 'that never betrayed me' – 'let me down' is, I believe, the modern expression.

One day when I had made a preposterously lucky 'hit' over a horse race, we were celebrating the occasion at dinner at the now-extinct St. James' Restaurant. I said to him, cheerily:

'Now, why can't you strike a streak of Fool's Luck like that?

'Well, Clement, my boy, I've a good mind to tell you. I have often thought of telling it to someone.'

I rather quailed. Was my ideal Colonel George going to confess some shady episode of the unknown past that was dogging his footsteps, embittering the present, and making the future ominous?

However, he changed the conversation, and after dinner he asked me to go back with him to his rooms – up near Regent's Park, a wretched place – instead of coming back to mine, and I did. When our pipes were lit, he sat looking at the empty fireplace for a little while, and then got up and went into his bedroom. When he returned he had in his hand the Nagpur Sapphire – the most splendid stone I had ever seen. I thought it was an amethyst but he told me no, it was a purple Sapphire – jewellers sometimes call them 'Oriental Amethysts.'

Here in the M.S. follows a long description of the stone and of its setting, practically as the Professor of Mineralogy has given it above.

C.B.

I said to him:

'You don't leave this about, do you, in a place like this?'

'Yes; it always lies about on my dressing table.'

'Aren't you afraid of having it stolen?'

'No; it has been stolen three times. I didn't get it back. I didn't want to. It came back. It always comes back.'

'What do you mean – you didn't want to?'

'I'd give all I possess to get rid of it. Instead of which, I have given all I possess for keeping it. This is 'the Curse of the Cardews.'

'My dear George,' I said, 'you are raving!'

'No, I am not; you asked me at dinner about my bad luck. Well, you hold it in your hand. That stone has ruined my whole family in turn.'

I protested. 'Such things only happen in books.'

'Listen to me. You know what a distinguished servant of 'John Company' my old father was. He looted that stone off a statue – an idol if you like – of Vishnú at Naghpúr, a stronghold of the Mutiny. The whole Shrine was razed to the ground by order; not a trace of it left. Next day he got his wound – one of those mysterious wounds that never heal – his never healed – it tortured him to his dying day. A month later he was on his way home – 'Invalided out of the Service' they said at home – but do you know what they said at the Secretariat in Calcutta?'

'No; what?'

'Cashiered for cowardice in face of the enemy.'

It was hushed up, first on account of his past services, and then on account of the probable effect upon the loyal native troops. On the way home his skull was fractured by a falling block – he was trephined and got over it, but his brain was never really clear again. You know how we lived down there in the little old house – pretty wretched, wasn't it? But what none of you knew was that my mother loathed the sight of my father – they never saw one another excepting in company. He was weak in the brain, as I said, but his nightmares were awful. I didn't know until afterwards that he was haunted by the phantom of an Indian yogi.'

As he paused, I put in, uneasily,

'Of course sick men do invent such things.'

'He didn't invent this one. It was the Attendant of the Shrine at Nagpur, whom he had cut down himself. And my governor knew that it was after the Purple Sapphire.'

'Why didn't he get rid of it?' George Cardew smiled.

'You have a short memory, Clement,' he said.

'I told you just now we can't get rid of it. The Governor sent it out by post to a man stationed near Nagpur and told him to restore it to the temple, or shrine, and if he couldn't do that, to sell it. It came back with the notification that there was no trace or record of the shrine, and the jewellers in the bazaars refused to buy, or even to touch it. My father sent it out again to another man, told him to bury it at Nagpur; six months later it came back by post – the man had buried it just as he received it with my father's letter – whoever dug it up got his address from that.'

'Why didn't he send it out without a letter to an imaginary address?'

'He did. It came back through the Dead Letter Office, straight to our village post office, and of course they knew there.'

'I'd have got rid of it somehow.'

'Would you? I'd like to see you try.'

A brilliant idea occurred to me.

'Give it to me,' I said, 'and I'll undertake to get rid of it.'

'You wait till you've heard the rest of it. When the old man died, and then my mother, it came to Dick. Well, you know what happened to him. I was at the zenith of my career when Dick died. Good God! Clement, my boy, but I was just on the point of stepping up to goodness knows where. And then I had to take over the Purple Sapphire.

'On hearing of Dick's death I spent eight pounds on a cablegram telling them to put it away, and on no account to send it out to me. I was too late – it had started. The day after he died – before he was buried – they sent it off. It arrived with his watch and chain and his shirt studs. The rest of his chattels only just paid for his funeral and a few small bills. Well, you know what happened to me. I had the bright idea to present it to my Maharajah, who had millions worth of gems. He refused it, and he began to mistrust and hate me from that day. I offered it to the Government Collection, but they looked upon it as a sort of attempted bribe to cover the mess I was making of things. I can't tell you what plans I made to get rid of it – scores – but it always came back, and there it is.'

He paused, and after lighting his pipe again, he smiled and said:

'Do you still want to have the damned thing?'

'Rather!' I said.

'You know my luck; it's impregnable.'

'Don't say that for Heaven's sake; it's an awful thing to say.'

'But I mean it,' I cried, 'I defy ill luck, and if I can't get the better of a mere stone.'

'Nobody ever will,' he interrupted, quite gravely.

We argued the matter for some time, and in the end I persuaded him. I took a cab home in the small hours, delighted with my splendid new toy.

Two years passed during which, personally, I was quite unaffected by any malevolent influence attributable to the Purple Sapphire, but I am bound to confess that there was something about it which passed comprehension and defied investigation.

To record an instance or two: I was deeply interested, as a hobby, in the elucidation of a curious text, half Persian and half Urdu, and a young Hindu scholar was sent to me by the Professor of Arabic and Persian in the University of Cosmopoli, with a view to the discussion of some obscure points, and to the augmentation of his income, and he arrived one evening about 8-30. He was called Mr Something Ghose, I remember. I had the books out on my study table, and we had been at them about half an hour, during which I thought Mr Ghose the most incompetent and absent-minded fraud I had ever met. At the end of that time he rose and said, with a little bow:

'You will excuse. I cannot work. I do not like this house. I go away.'

I was very much astonished, and not a little annoyed, and expressed myself with some succinctness. All he said was, as he made for the door:

'I am very sorry. I did not know. You must excuse. I go.'

And he went!

Shortly after this my friend the Professor of Arabic dined with me, always a delightful occasion for me, for he had been for many years Principal of a Muhammadan Madrassah in India, and was a delightful talker. As we sat before the fire smoking after dinner, I noticed that he looked all round the room at intervals, uneasily as it seemed to me. I said:

'Are you looking for anything?'

'No,' he replied. 'No; I don't think so. Tell me though, do you collect Indian curiosities?'

'No; I think them, as a rule, hideous.'

'You haven't got a Tirthankar in the house have you? One of those little squatting alabaster idols one sees in the curiosity shops?'

'No. I've seen hundreds of them and I hate them.'

'You are not far wrong,' replied the Professor, 'they're beastly things.'

'How?'

'Oh! they are uncanny things to have about,' and he changed the conversation.

Five minutes afterwards he looked round again, rose suddenly, and looking into the dark end of the room he exclaimed:

'I thought so! I felt it! Who are you? What do you want?'

'For heaven's sake, what's up?' I said.

'Haven't you seen that before! A Hindu squatting on his heels, naked excepting for a loincloth, scrabbling at the carpet – there in the corner?'

'My dear fellow,' I observed. 'I know you are not drunk, nor are you mad. What is it?'

He did not answer me at once, but extending his hand in the direction in which he was looking, he called sharply:

'Jao! Go away!'

He sat down again with a short laugh, and relit his pipe with a shaky hand.

'I don't wonder you are surprised,' he said. 'I'm sorry for this exhibition, but I've been so long in India; these things get into one's blood, I think. It's very stupid. You are sure you haven't got any Temple loot about the place? There's a lot of it about.'

I thought at once of the Purple Sapphire, and, rising, I took it from the drawer of my writing table and put it into his hand.

'Good Heavens!' he said.

'Of course this is it. This is what he is after. It's the pectoral gem of a Hindu God. Where did you get it? And how long have you had it?' I gave him an outline sketch of the history of the Purple Sapphire – which he had put down on the table by his side – and when I had finished he said:

'Of course that explains it – if anything can be said to explain the inexplicable. My advice to you, my earnest advice, is to get rid of this thing as quickly as you can.'

'Why?' Because – for goodness' sake never tell anyone of this incident or of this conversation – it will hurt you – smash you, sooner or later.'

We spent the rest of the evening in a most grizzly conversation. The Professor told me a number of stories in point, and if I had been an imaginative or nervous person I should have been very much upset.

But I am not, and I wasn't.

That was the last time the Professor dined with me until afterwards.

There were other such incidents, greater or lesser in degree, but I never saw any Yogi, and suffered no ill effects from being the custodian of the Purple Sapphire, which gradually acquired a romantic and rather fearsome interest among my friends.

I pass on to the night when I gave a dinner party which we shall all of us remember to our dying days.

We were eight – B. a rising young author; and a charming young actress Miss C., of whom he was the temporary 'enamourite,' to quote Burton; his sister, and G., a man in the Foreign Office, asked on account of one another; Mrs – I will call her Smith, as she comes back into the story later on under tragic and unforgettable circumstances; and Mrs A. and her husband Mrs A. was an odd woman. It might be said that she had not an enemy in the world, but was rather disliked by all her friends. She dabbled in Occultism and led her rather sheepish husband reluctantly to séances. She liked to flatter herself that she was 'a strong Medium.' She interested me, but I always regarded her as a fraud – a semiconscious fraud perhaps.

We had a jolly dinner, and afterwards congregated in the library.

Mrs. A., as usual, forced the conversation upon the Occult. She talked very well, and was always rather 'thrilling' to people who had not heard it all before.

B. said suddenly:

'I say, Arkwright, haven't you got a wonderful jewel or something that evokes spooks, and murders people in their sleep?'

At once there was a chorus of delighted curiosity, and finally I produced the purple Sapphire, which sparkled with remarkable vividness that night. At that moment one of those things that happen to the electric light happened – it is, I believe, when they change the accumulators or the dynamo at the generating station. At any rate the lights went down to about half their normal candlepower.

The Purple Sapphire seemed to flame even more brilliantly in the subdued light.

'Oh! Do give it to me,' exclaimed Miss C.

And with a view to making light of the whole thing I tossed it into her lap. She immediately held her hands up and away from it, as if it had been a spider or a mouse, and shrieked to B., who was sitting beside her,

'Take it away! Take it away!'

B. picked it out of her lap and handed it back to me. After this she sat closer to him for the rest of the evening, holding one of his hands in both of hers.

'Give it to me,' said Mrs A. in her most impressive tone, 'I am accustomed to these things.'

I gave it to her and she laid it, with the cover-flaps open, on her knee. She began to yarn about 'maleficent talismans,' but the evening was spoilt. We were all uneasy. Mrs Smith alone did not say a word, but sat looking at the Purple Sapphire and at me, in turns. Presently the preliminary murmurs of impending departure arose, and then some amazing things happened. Mrs A. leaned back in her chair and closed her eyes.

Then she cried out:

'Something is coming. Something is here! Everybody except Sir Clement go out of the room.'

They all sprang to their feet and scuttled into the hall.

Mrs A. said in a stifled voice,

'Oh, God!' and fainted.

At that moment the disturbance at the main righted itself and the electric lights blazed up again. I went to the door and called A.

'Your wife has fainted,' I said; 'come in.'

He came in, and with him Mrs Smith, uninvited. The rest were whispering together in the hall.

Mrs A's eyes were now open, and she said,

'It fell upon me, it fell through me.'

With one hand she was still holding the Purple Sapphire on her knee. We comforted and reassured her as best we could, but she declared that something had fallen into her lap and disappeared.

'It went through me,' she said, over and over again.

We got her onto her feet, and to prove to her that she was mistaken we pushed back the low armchair in which she had been sitting.

On the floor beneath it lay a small scarlet disc, faintly luminous in the strong light, about two and a half inches in diameter, on which were figured in black, exactly as on the flat flap of the Purple Sapphire, the Sign and Letters of the Tau!

We all gazed at it, horror-struck.

I was the first to pull myself together. I got the tongs from the fireplace, with a confused idea of picking the thing up, and flinging it into the fire! But even as we four looked at it, it turned white and clear of markings, and appeared to volatilize.

The others came in – and then they went away.

As a newspaper report would say 'the meeting broke up in confusion.' They did not all go away though; Mrs Smith remained. I may say at once that around this lady for some time all my thoughts had been concentrated. I shall write of her again.

We talked, she and I, long into the night. At 2 a.m. a ring came at the front door and I opened it. It was B. He said:

'What am I to do with Marie C.? She won't go home. We have been driving all over London in a hansom. She's there now, outside. She says she dare not go home to her rooms alone. Damn your infernal stone.'

I might have remarked that it was he who had insisted on its entry upon the scene. I forbore, however, and in the end Mrs Smith came out and took Miss C. home to her house to sleep with her. B. walked home, and I went to bed, I confess, rather shaken up. As Mrs. Smith left, she put her hands on my shoulders, and looked into my eyes searchingly. The others had gone outside.

'Didn't you see the Indian Man squatting on the floor behind Mrs A's chair?

'No, I didn't.'

'I swear to you he was there. Please don't go back and sit in the library. Promise me.'

I promised her – indeed, I do not think anything would have induced me to do so. As I say, I went to bed.

I was out to lunch next day, and on my return home I found a letter waiting for me, delivered by P.O. Express. It was from A. In it he wrote:

'I feel that I must send you the sequel to last night's extraordinary occurrences. About 3 a.m. my wife woke me, and said that something was burning her where the jewel had lain upon her knee. I tried to soothe her to sleep but she insisted so strongly that we switched on the light, and turned down the bedclothes. Sure enough, those letters around a capital T were burnt black upon, and through, her nightgown. We cut out the piece and I enclose it herewith – and on her leg, exactly the same thing, bright red, as if done with a hot iron. We dressed it with petroleum jelly, but it is there this morning. We will show it to you when you like.'

To avoid returning to this matter I may say that Mrs A. wears this brand to this day. She makes no bones about showing it to people, and I need hardly say that her account of my dinner party does not lose in the telling. Her enemies say she did it herself with a red-hot needle. Her husband says that he always knows, when she puts on her daintiest lingerie, that she is going to tell someone the story of the Purple Sapphire – as far as she knows it.

I now reach the dark and terrible part of my record. I have intimated that I was deeply devoted to Mrs Smith, who was one of the most beautiful, the cleverest, and by virtue of her husband's wealth, one of the most fastidiously luxurious women in London Society – which was literally at her feet – which were exquisite!

We had a vast community of interest, and were as inseparable as a decent regard for conventionality permitted us to be. I do not think I flatter myself when I say that I must have been a relief after her husband.

As to that gentleman, I was, and am, no doubt, prejudiced, but he combined in himself the millionaire, the lout, the drunkard, and the fool. I was ultra-careful never to compromise Mrs Smith in any way, for, as I repeatedly warned her, I would not have trusted her husband out of my sight for a moment, and was always prepared for him to lay some dirty trap or other for her. He encouraged our friendship, however, and threw us together continually. Timeo Danaos!

It made me therefore very uncomfortable and very unhappy when Cecile, at our next meeting after my dinner party next day, implored me to give her the Purple Sapphire. Though I had no fear of the thing for myself, I was frankly horror-struck at the idea of its passing into her possession.

She argued with me – how she argued!

'You brag about your invariable luck,' she said. 'Well, look at me, am I not the luckiest woman in London by common consent – in everything but my marriage. Am I not brave? Then why do you want me to be a coward? I thought you were brave. Then why are you a coward now? You do not believe the thing is bewitched. Then why do you behave like this now? I have never asked you for anything since we first met, have I? And now that I do beg a gift of you, you refuse it. Be very sure, my friend, that I shall never under any circumstances ask you for anything again. No, not if I were starving in the gutter.'

These words came back to me most bitterly when she was starving in the gutter, and when she did come to me for help. But what was I to do? One is only flesh and blood after all, and in certain circumstances 'Ce que femme veut – !' In the end I gave her the Purple Sapphire.

I will pass as quickly as I can over the miserable history which followed.

Men and women of my generation have not forgotten the Splendour and Decadence of Cecile Smith. In a phrase, everything went wrong with her. Her whole nature changed, she became hard, reckless, unsympathetic.

She gambled frenetically and lost vast sums; she got money to pay her debts by every means, fair and foul; she bought fabulous jewels, her transactions with which would have landed her in gaol had not her friends accommodated the situations into which she recklessly flung herself.

People whispered of lovers of low degree, of orgies, of drink, of drugs, of all the degenerate horrors of a decadent civilization. And meanwhile Smith was on the watch, to jerk the rope when she had had rope enough to hang a score of women.

This was not the affair of a moment – it took two years. All that time, though we seldom met now, for our paths had widely separated, I was continually imploring her to give me back the Purple Sapphire. I believed in it fundamentally at last. But she would not. She clung to it with a superstitious obstinacy.

In a letter from St. Petersburg where she had drifted as partner in a gambling enterprise, which failed of course, she wrote:

'The Stone is the last thing I had when I was queen of my race – and I was a queen! It is the only thing I ever asked you for. Nothing shall part me from it. P.S. – The yogi is here all right; thank God he costs nothing for railway fares and hotel expenses.'

Once, in reply to a passionate appeal for money from Madrid, I offered her £1,000 for it. Same result.

Time went on.

We heard of her occasionally – twice that she was in prison. I was very unhappy about her, worn out indeed, but there was nothing to be done.

To distract my thoughts I went an aimless voyage round the world, on which I met the lady who is now my wife. I returned to England, passing through Paris. I read to my horror that an unknown woman who had shot herself in a tenement house in La Vilette a few weeks before, had now been identified as the once beautiful and notorious Mrs Smith of London, Paris, Rome, St. Petersburg – and where not?

It was a ghastly shock, and in spite of the light that was breaking on my own horizon, I returned to London a sad and distracted man. A huge correspondence awaited me that my Secretary had been incompetent to deal with in my absence.

Among the heap was an official packet – it was from our Consul in Paris.

The letter said:

'The enclosed packet, sealed up and addressed to you, was found among the effects of the late Mrs. Smith who, as you may have heard, died recently in this city, in tragic circumstances. Kindly acknowledge,' etc. etc.

It was the Purple Sapphire.

Wrapped round it was a slip of paper on which Cecile had written:

'It has downed me – take it back. I have tried to sell it, but no one will buy it. Even thieves won't have it. Sayonara. Ave atque vale! Cecile.'

And so it came back.

A month later when I had settled down, burglars got into my house, and carried off property of great value, including the Purple Sapphire. They left me on the floor of my dining room with a bullet in my neck which all but closed my earthly record.

As soon as I was convalescent – that is to say about six weeks afterwards – I found that the burglars had been apprehended as the result of another burglary, the last of a long series perpetrated by this particular gang, which had hitherto completely baffled the police. Their mastermind had had a serious accident when on a professional tour, and had been arrested; the rest of the gang fell out among themselves, and partly by treachery and partly by mismanagement, the burglary for which they were awaiting trial, which had been postponed for my evidence, proved to be their last. It was the only beneficent action which can be laid to the score of the Purple Sapphire.

After these unhappy men had been sentenced, the solicitor in charge of the defence handed me a small packet.

I knew, without asking, what it was.

He accompanied the restoration with the words:

'My clients instructed me to return this to you. It is the only one of your jewels which they were unable to dispose of. They attribute – you know criminals are notoriously superstitious solely to it the unfortunate position in which they find themselves today. It was, in fact, their unaccountably rash efforts to get rid of it that gave the police the clue they have been seeking for a year past.'

And so it came back, and from that moment things began to go wrong all around me. My power to control the Purple Sapphire was gone. My solicitor absconded with a loss to me of several thousands of pounds which he had in his hands for investment. I also broke a leg and a collarbone riding along a simple country path. I spare you the rest of the catalogue of disasters, major and minor. They were many and varied.

I set about the task of getting rid of the Purple Sapphire. I sold it to a second-hand jeweller in Wardour Street who knew me well, but did not the less on that account offer me the value of a common Scotch amethyst of the same size. A week later he brought it back saying that his wife, who was Scotch, to whom he had given it would not have it in the house; she had a 'scunner' on it. I pawned it for £2. A month later the pawnbroker failed, and his trustee in bankruptcy sent it back to me 'as the sum for which it had been pledged was obviously inadequate, and he felt it his duty,' etc., etc.

Finally I took it to the National Museum of Cosmopoli, and offered it as a gift to the Keeper of Jewels. He turned it over and over, looking at me curiously, as I thought, and then said:

'This is a marvellous jewel – we have nothing like it – and you may think it odd, but I don't think we want it.'

'For Heaven's sake, why?' I asked.

'You will think it odd, but I am a firm believer in the malevolence of certain stones which have been the witnesses or causes of tragedies. I am convinced that this is one of them. Why do you want to get rid of it?'

There was no help for it – I was too broken in spirit – I told him.

He listened very attentively and when I had finished, with a suggestion that I should smash it up and scatter the fragments, he said:

'No, don't do that. As it is, you know it, you can recognise it, and can be on your guard; if you smash it, it will come back to you, somehow, in pieces, re-cut, that you will not recognise, and you may unconsciously hurt someone. Now do not think that I am mad –though I admit that my colleagues in the Museum think I am, to say the least of it, eccentric upon this subject – but you must follow the direction of the old books on Magic and Witchcraft; there is much more in them than most people think, or will admit. You must drop this into a tidal river at the exact moment of dead high water; it is the only thing you can do, and I warn you that even that may fail.'

I confess I felt extraordinarily relieved at the suggestion; this surely must be final! We got out a Nautical Almanack and calculated the time of dead high water in the Thames on a particular day, and on that day and at that minute I dropped the Purple Sapphire into the river from the middle of Charing Cross Bridge.

All went well with me for about three months.

The happiness I had seen approaching on my world tour seemed well on its way to realization. My nerves regained their equilibrium. Life was once more worth living.

Then one day as I was working in my library my parlour maid announced:

'A man with a note from Mr. X.'

This was my jeweller friend in Wardour Street.

The note said:

'The bearer has a curious jewel for sale which was once in your possession. I do not know how he may have come by it, but I send him to you as you may care to re-purchase the article, of which he does not know the value, or to hand him over to the police.'

I looked up, and the man, a common working 'navvy' produced from a wrapping of dirty rag, the Purple Sapphire.

I was stunned. I sat looking stupidly at the accursed thing, and it seemed to me as if someone else's voice said to the man:

'Where did you get this from?'

He began a whining rigmarole. It been in his family from father to son for many generations; they had come down in the world. He had come to London to seek work, had got it – good work, highly paid, but he had lost it, luck had turned against him, one of his children had died, his wife was ill, they were starving. At last, with great reluctance they had decided to sell the old 'amethyst' –that's what his father had said it was. Worth lots of money. He had taken it to Mr X., and Mr X. had sent him to me as I was a gent who gave good money for curios.

My interruption startled him. I sprang to my feet and shouted at him:

'You liar!'

'Come, governor, none of that. Give me back my curio.'

'Not till I've got the truth out of you. If you try to get away I'll give you to the policeman outside. Now then, out with it. How did you get this out of the bed of the Thames?'

He fell into a chair as if he had been shot, stammering.

'Christ! It's witchcraft, that's what it is. Devils and that. It's just bloody witchcraft.'

'You see,' said I, 'I know something. You had better tell me the rest.'

It took him several minutes to recover his normal self, and then he told me. It was amazing. The extraordinary network of underground railways – 'the Tubes' they came to be called, later was just then beginning to be constructed. One of them passed under the Thames from Charing Cross to Waterloo Station. This man was employed in the caissons the river mud, pushing forward foot by foot in compressed air chambers, digging out the river bed and passing the debris back to shore. He had caught the glint of this thing in one of the scoops as it came home, and watching his opportunity, he 'pinched it – and pouched it.'

'I give you my word, governor,' the wretch went on, 'I've never had a good since. It's the first thing ever I pinched, and it's got back on me. I've to sell it – no one will buy it from the likes of me. I've tried to lose it – it's brought back to me. I believe the police is after me on account of it. For Gawd's sake Mister take it off my hands.'

My heart went out to the poor devil.

'I know the stone,' I said. 'I lost it. I'll take it back. Here's a fiver for you. Go home and good luck to you. You'll get along better now.'

His gratitude was pathetic.

'I feel better already, governor,' he said.

'Gawd knows it'll be a lesson to me.'

And so it came back.

I knew now that any effort of mine to get rid of it would be in vain, and I decided that after all it would be better to know where it was, than to dispose of it and feel that any day or hour it might turn up again.

So I wrapped it up in the piece of Indian muslin in which George Cardew had given it to me and put it into its nest of boxes. I have forgotten, in writing this, to record that shortly after Colonel George made it over to me, he sent me a 'nest' of seven sandal-wood boxes of Indian make, fitting closely inside one another, the smallest and innermost of which exactly held the Purple Sapphire. Whether he, or his father, or Dr. Dick had them made I never knew, or if I did, I have forgotten. I then wrote a note of instruction to the executors of my will directing that the Purple Sapphire should not see the light of day until twenty-five years had elapsed after my death. I little supposed that by that time its power for evil would have, so to speak, evaporated, but at any rate I could make sure that it should not fall into the hands of my children until they were old enough to have read this manuscript and to judge for themselves what was the next thing to be done with it.

The Professor of Mineralogy has transcribed this letter of instructions in the early sheets of his record, so it is not necessary to repeat it here. – C.B. With a view to enforcing the performance of my wish I set aside by my will a sum of £10,000, the income of which followed my residuary estate, with a provision that, in the event of the parcel having been opened before the prescribed time, the capital sum was to be transferred at once to one of our larger hospitals.

I felt that the Governors of that hospital would keep an eye upon the parcel and see from time to time that it was intact. At the end of the twenty-five years the £10,000 is to fall into residue. I wrapped up and sealed the parcel and took it to my bankers, where I deposited it for safe custody in their vaults.

The manager, a charming man and a personal friend of mine, received it in the ordinary way, and I need hardly say that I did not give him any inkling of its contents or of my motives for the deposit. Whether it was a coincidence, or otherwise, I cannot tell, but from that moment the affairs of that branch of my bank went wrong in many ways.

One of the cashiers absconded with a large sum of money, loans which the bank had made went wrong, commercial houses which they had financed failed and involved them in heavy losses, and of course the manager got the blame, and he was forced into retirement on a small pension, a broken and disappointed man. I had my own uncomfortable ideas on the subject, but it is obvious that I could not go to the head office and say it was all my fault for having deposited in the vaults a parcel containing the Purple Sapphire. They would rightly have assumed that my brain was softening.

And there it lies to this day. I am happily married and I have two charming children, a girl and a boy. I sometimes wonder whether it will be he, or his son, upon whom will devolve the awful responsibility of taking the Purple Sapphire from its resting place.

Clement Arkwright.

31st December, 18 –.'

***

The manuscript of Sir Clement Arkwright stopped here.

He lived for many years after the date which he appended. There follows in the notebook a further entry in another hand which reads:

'1st January, 1920. The twenty-five years since the death of my brother expired yesterday, and I went to the bank and claimed the parcel, which we found – the manager and I – dusty but intact. I opened it in his presence and read the letter of instructions, but I did not open the sandalwood boxes. I am not superstitious, but somehow I – well, at any rate I did not open them.

We wrapped up and re-sealed the parcel and left it again where it had lain for over forty years. I must record, by way of postscript to my brother's account, a curious, and to me very ominous, circumstance.

During the Great War the staff of the bank, those of military age that is to say, had been largely replaced by women, several of whom are still in the employ of the bank. As the manager was seeing me to the door I said to him:

'I suppose you will be gradually getting rid of these young ladies?'

'Yes,' replied he, 'and I shall be very glad when we see the last of them.

'One can never rely upon their work, their hearts are not in it for they know that it is not their life's work and that they can never rise to the administrative grades in the service. They make the most annoying mistakes, and one has to have their work continually checked by the men. And as a culminating touch, what do you think? There is a mad idea among them that makes them absolutely refuse to go down into the vaults when we want to send for anything. They say the vaults are haunted! Two of them declared that they had seen an apparition of a naked Indian who grinned and gibbered at them down there. Did you ever hear of such hysterical idiocy? Oh I shall be glad to get rid of them.'

'I said nothing beyond what might be conventionally expected of me, but I drove home feeling very uncomfortable.

'Is this horrible thing, after lying quiet for forty years, going to wake into renewed activity? I suppose I ought to deliver it to my nephew and godson Sir Gilbert Arkwright, but frankly I am afraid to do so. Fortunately he is still abroad, in the Army of Occupation in Germany. I shall let matters rest as they are until he comes home. Gilbert Arkwright.'

Following upon this was a further entry in the same hand which reads as follows:

'23rd June, 1920. My nephew Gilbert has returned home, and I have made him read this record in his father's hand. He is a splendid fellow and he laughs, of course, at the whole thing. 'At any rate,' he said, 'let us take it out and have a look at it.' I begged him not to insist upon anything of the kind, and at last, after many long arguments, which I fear have convinced him that I am suffering from senile decay, he has consented to the plan which I have proposed. This is, that I should take the parcel just as it is to the Professor of Mineralogy in the University of Cosmopoli and present it to the university Museum. It may be presumed – or at least hoped – that, placed among a large collection, many specimens in which may possibly have histories no less mysterious than that of the Purple Sapphire, its evil powers may be as it were diluted, if not dissipated. In any case, I take it to the University tomorrow, and there I sincerely trust that, so far as our family is concerned, the history of the Purple Sapphire is at an end. Gilbert Arkwright.'

***

It was very late when I had finished reading through the pages of the black notebook.

The handwriting of the main record left much to be desired in places, having evidently been written under the influence of strong emotion. And no wonder! I felt that the writer was compelling himself to a violent effort all the time, omitting much, passing lightly over incidents which it must have been very painful for him to record. I pitied him from the bottom of my heart.

Next day I went up into the Museum and looked at the Purple Sapphire. There it lay, appropriately labelled:

'Sapphire (Purple) Alumina. Corundum. Refraction, 86°4′ Hardness, 9. Sp.gr. 3.9. – 4.16.' A bald description of what is perhaps the most remarkable stone in the collection.

There is no reason why any student should ever refer to the little black notebook, but I do sometimes wonder whether anyone, browsing among the shelves of the library, will ever take it down and read these records.

And then I wonder many things.

The $30,000 Bequest

Chapter I

Lakeside was a pleasant little town of five or six thousand inhabitants, and a rather pretty one, too, as towns go in the Far West. It had church accommodations for thirty-five thousand, which is the way of the Far West and the South, where everybody is religious, and where each of the Protestant sects is represented and has a plant of its own. Rank was unknown in Lakeside – unconfessed, anyway; everybody knew everybody and his dog, and a sociable friendliness was the prevailing atmosphere.

Saladin Foster was bookkeeper in the principal store, and the only high-salaried man of his profession in Lakeside. He was thirty-five years old, now; he had served that store for fourteen years; he had begun in his marriage week at four hundred dollars a year, and had climbed steadily up, a hundred dollars a year, for four years; from that time forth his wage had remained eight hundred – a handsome figure indeed, and everybody conceded that he was worth it.

His wife, Electra, was a capable helpmeet, although –
like himself – a dreamer of dreams and a private dabbler
in romance. The first thing she did, after her marriage –
child as she was, aged only nineteen – was to buy an acre of
ground on the edge of the town, and pay down the cash for
it – twenty-five dollars, all her fortune. Saladin had less, by
fifteen. She instituted a vegetable garden there, got it farmed
on shares by the nearest neighbour, and made it pay her a
hundred per cent a year.

Out of Saladin's first year's wage she put thirty dollars
in the savings bank, sixty out of his second, a hundred
out of his third, a hundred and fifty out of his fourth. His
wage went to eight hundred a year, then, and meantime two
children had arrived and increased the expenses, but she
banked two hundred a year from the salary, nevertheless,
thenceforth. When she had been married seven years she
built and furnished a pretty and comfortable two-thousand-
dollar house in the midst of her garden-acre, paid half of the
money down and moved her family in. Seven years later she
was out of debt and had several hundred dollars out earning
its living.

Earning it by the rise in landed estate; for she had long ago
bought another acre or two and sold the most of it at a profit
to pleasant people who were willing to build, and would
be good neighbours and furnish a general comradeship for
herself and her growing family. She had an independent
income from safe investments of about a hundred dollars a
year; her children were growing in years and grace; and she
was a pleased and happy woman. Happy in her husband,

happy in her children, and the husband and the children were happy in her. It is at this point that this history begins.

The youngest girl, Clytemnestra – called Clytie for short – was eleven; her sister, Gwendolen – called Gwen for short – was thirteen; nice girls, and comely. The names betray the latent romance tinge in the parental blood, the parents' names indicate that the tinge was an inheritance. It was an affectionate family, hence all four of its members had pet names, Saladin's was a curious and unsexing one – Sally; and so was Electra's – Aleck. All day long Sally was a good and diligent bookkeeper and salesman; all day long Aleck was a good and faithful mother and housewife, and thoughtful and calculating businesswoman; but in the cozy living room at night they put the plodding world away, and lived in another and a fairer, reading romances to each other, dreaming dreams, comrading with kings and princes and stately lords and ladies in the flash and stir and splendour of noble palaces and grim and ancient castles.

Chapter II

Now came great news! Stunning news – joyous news, in fact. It came from a neighbouring state, where the family's only surviving relative lived. It was Sally's relative – a sort of vague and indefinite uncle or second or third cousin by the name of Tilbury Foster, seventy and a bachelor, reputed well off and corresponding sour and crusty. Sally had tried to make up to him once, by letter, in a bygone time, and had not made that mistake again. Tilbury now wrote to Sally, saying he should shortly die, and should leave him thirty thousand dollars, cash; not for love, but because money had given him most of his troubles and exasperations, and he wished to place it where there was good hope that it would continue its malignant work. The bequest would be found in his will, and would be paid over. PROVIDED, that Sally should be able to prove to the executors that he had *Taken no notice of the gift by spoken word or by letter, had made no inquiries concerning the moribund's progress toward the everlasting tropics, and had not attended the funeral.*

As soon as Aleck had partially recovered from the tremendous emotions created by the letter, she sent to the relative's habitat and subscribed for the local paper.

Man and wife entered into a solemn compact, now, to never mention the great news to anyone while the relative lived, lest some ignorant person carry the fact to the death-bed and distort it and make it appear that they were disobediently thankful for the bequest, and just the same as confessing it and publishing it, right in the face of the prohibition.

For the rest of the day Sally made havoc and confusion with his books, and Aleck could not keep her mind on her affairs, not even take up a flower pot or book or a stick of wood without forgetting what she had intended to do with it. For both were dreaming.

'Thirty thousand dollars!'

All day long the music of those inspiring words sang through those people's heads.

From his marriage day forth, Aleck's grip had been upon the purse, and Sally had seldom known what it was to be privileged to squander a dime on non-necessities.

'Thirty thousand dollars!' the song went on and on. A vast sum, an unthinkable sum!

All day long Aleck was absorbed in planning how to invest it, Sally in planning how to spend it.

There was no romance-reading that night. The children took themselves away early, for their parents were silent, distraught, and strangely unentertaining. The good-night kisses might as well have been impressed upon vacancy, for all the response they got; the parents were not aware of the kisses, and the children had been gone an hour before their absence was noticed. Two pencils had been busy during that hour – note-making; in the way of plans. It was Sally who broke the stillness at last. He said, with exultation:

'Ah, it'll be grand, Aleck! Out of the first thousand we'll have a horse and a buggy for summer, and a cutter and a skin lap-robe for winter.'

Aleck responded with decision and composure –

'Out of the *capital*? Nothing of the kind. Not if it was a million!'

Sally was deeply disappointed; the glow went out of his face.

'Oh, Aleck!' he said, reproachfully. 'We've always worked so hard and been so scrimped: and now that we are rich, it does seem – '

He did not finish, for he saw her eye soften; his supplication had touched her. She said, with gentle persuasiveness:

'We must not spend the capital, dear, it would not be wise. Out of the income from it – '

'That will answer, that will answer, Aleck! How dear and good you are! There will be a noble income and if we can spend that – '

'Not *all* of it, dear, not all of it, but you can spend a part of it. That is, a reasonable part. But the whole of the capital – every penny of it – must be put right to work, and kept at it. You see the reasonableness of that, don't you?'

'Why, ye-s. Yes, of course. But we'll have to wait so long. Six months before the first interest falls due.'

'Yes – maybe longer.'

'Longer, Aleck? Why? Don't they pay half-yearly?'

'*That* kind of an investment – yes; but I shan't invest in that way.'

'What way, then?'

'For big returns.'

'Big. That's good. Go on, Aleck. What is it?'

'Coal. The new mines. Cannel. I mean to put in ten thousand. Ground floor. When we organize, we'll get three shares for one.'

'By George, but it sounds good, Aleck! Then the shares will be worth – how much? And when?'

'About a year. They'll pay ten per cent half-yearly, and be worth thirty thousand. I know all about it; the advertisement is in the Cincinnati paper here.'

'Land, thirty thousand for ten – in a year! Let's jam in the whole capital and pull out ninety! I'll write and subscribe right now – tomorrow it may be too late.'

He was flying to the writing desk, but Aleck stopped him and put him back in his chair. She said:

'Don't lose your head so. *We* mustn't subscribe till we've got the money; don't you know that?'

Sally's excitement went down a degree or two, but he was not wholly appeased.

'Why, Aleck, we'll *have* it, you know – and so soon, too. He's probably out of his troubles before this; it's a hundred to nothing he's selecting his brimstone shovel this very minute. Now, I think – '

Aleck shuddered, and said:

'How *can* you, Sally! Don't talk in that way, it is perfectly scandalous.'

'Oh, well, make it a halo, if you like, *I* don't care for his outfit, I was only just talking. Can't you let a person talk?'

'But why should you *want* to talk in that dreadful way? How would you like to have people talk so about *you*, and you not cold yet?'

'Not likely to be, for *one* while, I reckon, if my last act was giving away money for the sake of doing somebody a harm with it. But never mind about Tilbury, Aleck, let's talk about something worldly. It does seem to me that that mine is the place for the whole thirty. What's the objection?'

'All the eggs in one basket – that's the objection.'

'All right, if you say so. What about the other twenty? What do you mean to do with that?'

'There is no hurry; I am going to look around before I do anything with it.'

'All right, if your mind's made up,' sighed Sally. He was deep in thought awhile, then he said:

'There'll be twenty thousand profit coming from the ten a year from now. We can spend that, can't we, Aleck?'

Aleck shook her head.

'No, dear,' she said, 'it won't sell high till we've had the first semi-annual dividend. You can spend part of that.'

'Shucks, only *that* – and a whole year to wait! Confound it, I... '

'Oh, do be patient! It might even be declared in three months – it's quite within the possibilities.'

'Oh, jolly! Oh, thanks!' and Sally jumped up and kissed his wife in gratitude.

'It'll be three thousand – three whole thousand! how much of it can we spend, Aleck? Make it liberal! – Do, dear, that's a good fellow.'

Aleck was pleased; so pleased that she yielded to the pressure and conceded a sum which her judgment told her was a foolish extravagance – a thousand dollars. Sally kissed her half a dozen times and even in that way could not express all his joy and thankfulness. This new access of gratitude and affection carried Aleck quite beyond the bounds of prudence, and before she could restrain herself she had made her darling another grant – a couple of thousand out of the fifty or sixty which she meant to clear within a year of the twenty which still remained of the bequest. The happy tears sprang to Sally's eyes, and he said:

'Oh, I want to hug you!'

And he did it. Then he got his notes and sat down and began to check off, for first purchase, the luxuries which he should earliest wish to secure.

'Horse – buggy – cutter – lap-robe – patent-leathers – dog – plug-hat – church-pew – stem-winder – new teeth – *say*, Aleck!'

'Well?'

'Ciphering away, aren't you? That's right. Have you got the twenty thousand invested yet?'

'No, there's no hurry about that; I must look around first, and think.'

'But you are ciphering; what's it about?'

'Why, I have to find work for the thirty thousand that comes out of the coal, haven't I?'

'Scott, what a head! I never thought of that. How are you getting along? Where have you arrived?'

'Not very far – two years or three. I've turned it over twice; once in oil and once in wheat.'

'Why, Aleck, it's splendid! How does it aggregate?'

'I think – well, to be on the safe side, about a hundred and eighty thousand clear, though it will probably be more.'

'My! Isn't it wonderful? By gracious! luck has come our way at last, after all the hard sledding. Aleck!'

'Well?'

'I'm going to cash in a whole three hundred on the missionaries – what real right have we care for expenses!'

'You couldn't do a nobler thing, dear; and it's just like your generous nature, you unselfish boy.'

The praise made Sally poignantly happy, but he was fair and just enough to say it was rightfully due to Aleck rather than to himself, since but for her he should never have had the money.

Then they went up to bed, and in their delirium of bliss they forgot and left the candle burning in the parlour. They did not remember until they were undressed; then Sally was for letting it burn; he said they could afford it, if it was a thousand. But Aleck went down and put it out.

A good job, too; for on her way back she hit on a scheme that would turn the hundred and eighty thousand into half a million before it had had time to get cold.

Chapter III

The little newspaper which Aleck had subscribed for was a Thursday sheet; it would make the trip of five hundred miles from Tilbury's village and arrive on Saturday. Tilbury's letter had started on Friday, more than a day too late for the benefactor to die and get into that week's issue, but in plenty of time to make connection for the next output. Thus the Fosters had to wait almost a complete week to find out whether anything of a satisfactory nature had happened to him or not. It was a long, long week, and the strain was a heavy one. The pair could hardly have borne it if their minds had not had the relief of wholesome diversion. We have seen that they had that. The woman was piling up fortunes right along, the man was spending them – spending all his wife would give him a chance at, at any rate.

At last the Saturday came, and the *Weekly Sagamore* arrived. Mrs. Eversly Bennett was present. She was the Presbyterian parson's wife, and was working the

Fosters for a charity. Talk now died a sudden death – on the Foster side. Mrs. Bennett presently discovered that her hosts were not hearing a word she was saying; so she got up, wondering and indignant, and went away. The moment she was out of the house, Aleck eagerly tore the wrapper from the paper, and her eyes and Sally's swept the columns for the death notices. Disappointment! Tilbury was not anywhere mentioned. Aleck was a Christian from the cradle, and duty and the force of habit required her to go through the motions. She pulled herself together and said, with a pious two-per cent trade joyousness:

'Let us be humbly thankful that he has been spared; and… '

'Damn his treacherous hide, I wish… '

'Sally! For shame!'

'I don't care!' retorted the angry man.

'It's the way *you* feel, and if you weren't so immorally pious you'd be honest and say so.'

Aleck said, with wounded dignity:

'I do not see how you can say such unkind and unjust things. There is no such thing as immoral piety.'

Sally felt a pang, but tried to conceal it under a shuffling attempt to save his case by changing the form of it – as if changing the form while retaining the juice could deceive the expert he was trying to placate. He said:

'I didn't mean so bad as that, Aleck; I didn't really mean immoral piety, I only meant – meant – well, conventional piety, you know; er – shop piety; the – the – why, *you* know what I mean. Aleck – the – well, where you put up that plated article and play it for solid, you know, without intending

52

anything improper, but just out of trade habit, ancient policy, petrified custom, loyalty to – to – hang it, I can't find the right words, but *you* know what I mean, Aleck, and that there isn't any harm in it. I'll try again. You see, it's this way. If a person... '

'You have said quite enough,' said Aleck, coldly; 'let the subject be dropped.'

'I'm willing,' fervently responded Sally, wiping the sweat from his forehead and looking the thankfulness he had no words for. Then, musingly, he apologized to himself.

'I certainly held threes – *I know* it – but I drew and didn't fill. That's where I'm so often weak in the game. If I had stood pat – but I didn't. I never do. I don't know enough.'

Confessedly defeated, he was properly tame now and subdued. Aleck forgave him with her eyes.

The grand interest, the supreme interest, came instantly to the front again; nothing could keep it in the background many minutes on a stretch. The couple took up the puzzle of the absence of Tilbury's death notice. They discussed it every which way, more or less hopefully, but they had to finish where they began, and concede that the only really sane explanation of the absence of the notice must be – and without doubt was – that Tilbury was not dead. There was something sad about it, something even a little unfair, maybe, but there it was, and had to be put up with. They were agreed as to that. To Sally it seemed a strangely inscrutable dispensation; more inscrutable than usual, he thought; one of the most unnecessary inscrutable he could call to mind, in fact – and said so, with some feeling; but if he was hoping to draw Aleck he failed; she reserved her opinion, if she had one; she had not the habit of taking injudicious risks in any market, worldly or other.

The pair must wait for next week's paper – Tilbury had evidently postponed. That was their thought and their decision. So they put the subject away and went about their affairs again with as good heart as they could.

Now, if they had but known it, they had been wronging Tilbury all the time. Tilbury had kept faith, kept it to the letter; he was dead, he had died to schedule. He was dead more than four days now and used to it; entirely dead, perfectly dead, as dead as any other new person in the cemetery; dead in abundant time to get into that week's *Sagamore*, too, and only shut out by an accident; an accident which could not happen to a metropolitan journal, but which happens easily to a poor little village rag like the *Sagamore*. On this occasion, just as the editorial page was being locked up, a gratis quart of strawberry ice water arrived from Hostetter's Ladies and Gents Ice-Cream Parlours, and the stickful of rather chilly regret over Tilbury's translation got crowded out to make room for the editor's frantic gratitude.

On its way to the standing-galley Tilbury's notice got pied. Otherwise it would have gone into some future edition, for *Weekly Sagamores* do not waste 'live' matter, and in their galleys 'live' matter is immortal, unless a pi accident intervenes. But a thing that gets pied is dead, and for such there is no resurrection; its chance of seeing print is gone, forever and ever. And so, let Tilbury like it or not, let him rave in his grave to his fill, no matter – no mention of his death would ever see the light in the *Weekly Sagamore*.

Chapter IV

Five weeks drifted tediously along. The *Sagamore* arrived regularly on the Saturdays, but never once contained a mention of Tilbury Foster. Sally's patience broke down at this point, and he said, resentfully:

'Damn his livers, he's immortal!'

Aleck gave him a very severe rebuke, and added with icy solemnity:

'How would you feel if you were suddenly cut off just after such an awful remark had escaped out of you?'

Without sufficient reflection Sally responded:

'I'd feel I was lucky I hadn't got caught with it *in* me.'

Pride had forced him to say something, and as he could not think of any rational thing to say he flung that out. Then he stole a base – as he called it – that is, slipped from the presence, to keep from being brayed in his wife's discussion mortar.

Six months came and went. The *Sagamore* was still silent about Tilbury. Meantime, Sally had several times thrown out a feeler – that is, a hint that he would like to know. Aleck had ignored the hints. Sally now resolved to brace up and risk a frontal attack. So he squarely proposed to disguise himself and go to Tilbury's village and surreptitiously find out as to the prospects. Aleck put her foot on the dangerous project with energy and decision. She said:

'What can you be thinking of? You do keep my hands full! You have to be watched all the time, like a little child, to keep you from walking into the fire. You'll stay right where you are!'

'Why, Aleck, I could do it and not be found out – I'm certain of it.'

'Sally Foster, don't you know you would have to inquire around?'

'Of course, but what of it? Nobody would suspect who I was.'

'Oh, listen to the man! Someday you've got to prove to the executors that you never inquired. What then?'

He had forgotten that detail. He didn't reply; there wasn't anything to say. Aleck added:

'Now then, drop that notion out of your mind, and don't ever meddle with it again. Tilbury set that trap for you. Don't you know it's a trap? He is on the watch, and fully expecting you to blunder into it. Well, he is going to be disappointed – at least while I am on deck. Sally!'

'Well?'

'As long as you live, if it's a hundred years, don't you ever make an inquiry. Promise!'

'All right,' with a sigh and reluctantly.

Then Aleck softened and said:

'Don't be impatient. We are prospering; we can wait; there is no hurry. Our small dead-certain income increases all the time; and as to futures, I have not made a mistake yet – they are piling up by the thousands and tens of thousands. There is not another family in the state with such prospects as ours. Already we are beginning to roll in eventual wealth. You know that, don't you?'

'Yes, Aleck, it's certainly so.'

'Then be grateful for what God is doing for us and stop worrying. You do not believe we could have achieved these prodigious results without His special help and guidance, do you?'

Hesitatingly,

'N-no, I suppose not.'

Then, with feeling and admiration,

'And yet, when it comes to judiciousness in watering a stock or putting up a hand to skin Wall Street I don't give in that *you* need any outside amateur help, if I do wish I – '

'Oh, *do* shut up! I know you do not mean any harm or any irreverence, poor boy, but you can't seem to open your mouth without letting out things to make a person shudder. You keep me in constant dread. For you and for all of us. Once I had no fear of the thunder, but now when I hear it I – '

Her voice broke, and she began to cry, and could not finish. The sight of this smote Sally to the heart and he took her in his arms and petted her and comforted her and promised better conduct, and upbraided himself and remorsefully pleaded for forgiveness. And he was in earnest, and sorry for what he had done and ready for any sacrifice that could make up for it.

And so, in privacy, he thought long and deeply over the matter, resolving to do what should seem best. It was easy to *promise* reform; indeed he had already promised it. But would that do any real good, any permanent good? No, it would be but temporary – he knew his weakness, and confessed it to himself with sorrow – he could not keep the promise. Something surer and better must be devised; and he devised it. At cost of precious money which he had long been saving up, shilling by shilling, he put a lightning rod on the house.

At a subsequent time he relapsed.

What miracles habit can do! And how quickly and how easily habits are acquired – both trifling habits and habits which profoundly change us. If by accident we wake at two in the morning a couple of nights in succession, we have need to be uneasy, for another repetition can turn the accident into a habit; and a month's dallying with whiskey – but we all know these commonplace facts.

The castle-building habit, the daydreaming habit – how it grows! What a luxury it becomes; how we fly to its enchantments at every idle moment, how we revel in them, steep our souls in them, intoxicate ourselves with their beguiling fantasies – oh yes, and how soon and how easily our dream life and our material life become so intermingled and so fused together that we can't quite tell which is which, any more.

By and by Aleck subscribed to a Chicago daily and for the *Wall Street Pointer*. With an eye single to finance she studied these as diligently all the week as she studied her Bible Sundays. Sally was lost in admiration, to note with what swift and sure strides her genius and judgment developed and expanded in the forecasting and handling of the securities of both the material and spiritual markets.

He was proud of her nerve and daring in exploiting worldly stocks, and just as proud of her conservative caution in working her spiritual deals. He noted that she never lost her head in either case; that with a splendid courage she often went short on worldly futures, but heedfully drew the line there – she was always long on the others. Her policy was quite sane and simple, as she explained it to him: what she put into earthly futures was for speculation, what she put into spiritual futures was for investment; she was willing to go into the one on a margin, and take chances, but in the case of the other, 'margin her no margins' – she wanted to cash in a hundred cents per dollar's worth, and have the stock transferred on the books.

It took but a very few months to educate Aleck's imagination and Sally's. Each day's training added something to the spread and effectiveness of the two machines. As a consequence, Aleck made imaginary money much faster than at first she had dreamed of making it, and Sally's competency in spending the overflow of it kept pace with the strain put upon it, right along. In the beginning, Aleck had given the coal speculation a twelvemonth in which to materialize, and had been loath to grant that this term might possibly be shortened by nine months. But that was the feeble work, the nursery work, of a financial fancy that had had no teaching, no experience, no practice. These aids soon came, then that nine months vanished, and the imaginary ten-thousand-dollar investment came marching home with three hundred per cent profit on its back!

It was a great day for the pair of Fosters. They were speechless for joy. Also speechless for another reason: after much watching of the market, Aleck had lately, with fear and trembling, made her first flyer on a 'margin,' using the remaining twenty thousand of the bequest in this risk. In her mind's eye she had seen it climb, point by point – always with a chance that the market would break – until at last her anxieties were too great for further endurance – she being new to the margin business and unhardened, as yet – and she gave her imaginary broker an imaginary order by imaginary telegraph to sell. She said forty thousand dollars' profit was enough. The sale was made on the very day that the coal venture had returned with its rich freight. As I have said, the couple were speechless, they sat dazed and blissful that night, trying to realize that they were actually worth a hundred thousand dollars in clean, imaginary cash. Yet so it was.

It was the last time that ever Aleck was afraid of a margin; at least afraid enough to let it break her sleep and pale her cheek to the extent that this first experience in that line had done.

Indeed it was a memorable night. Gradually the realization that they were rich sank securely home into the souls of the pair, then they began to place the money. If we could have looked out through the eyes of these dreamers, we should have seen their tidy little wooden house disappear, and two-story brick with a cast-iron fence in front of it take its place; we should have seen a three-globed gas chandelier grow down from the parlour ceiling; we should have seen the homely rag carpet turn to noble Brussels, a dollar and a half a yard; we should have seen the plebeian fireplace vanish away and a recherche, big base-burner with isinglass windows take position and spread awe around. And we should have seen other things, too; among them the buggy, the lap-robe, the stove-pipe hat, and so on.

From that time forth, although the daughters and the neighbours saw only the same old wooden house there, it was a two-story brick to Aleck and Sally and not a night went by that Aleck did not worry about the imaginary gas-bills, and get for all comfort Sally's reckless retort:

'What of it? We can afford it.'

Before the couple went to bed, that first night that they were rich, they had decided that they must celebrate. They must give a party – that was the idea. But how to explain it – to the daughters and the neighbours? They could not expose the fact that they were rich. Sally was willing, even anxious, to do it; but Aleck kept her head and would not allow it. She said that although the money was as good as in, it would be as well to wait until it was actually in. On that policy she took her stand, and would not budge. The great secret must be kept, she said – kept from the daughters and everybody else.

The pair were puzzled. They must celebrate, they were determined to celebrate, but since the secret must be kept, what could they celebrate? No birthdays were due for three months. Tilbury wasn't available, evidently he was going to live forever; what the nation *could* they celebrate? That was Sally's way of putting it; and he was getting impatient, too, and harassed. But at last he hit it – just by sheer inspiration, as it seemed to him – and all their troubles were gone in a moment; they would celebrate the Discovery of America. A splendid idea!

Aleck was almost too proud of Sally for words – she said *she* never would have thought of it. But Sally, although he was bursting with delight in the compliment and with wonder at himself, tried not to let on, and said it wasn't really anything, anybody could have done it. Whereat Aleck, with a prideful toss of her happy head, said:

'Oh, certainly! Anybody could – oh, anybody! Hosannah Dilkins, for instance! Or maybe Adelbert Peanut – oh, *dear* – yes! Well, I'd like to see them try it, that's all. Dear-me-suz, if they could think of the discovery of a forty-acre island it's more than *I* believe they could; and as for the whole continent, why, Sally Foster, you know perfectly well it would strain the livers and lights out of them and *then* they couldn't!'

The dear woman, she knew he had talent; and if affection made her over-estimate the size of it a little, surely it was a sweet and gentle crime, and forgivable for its source's sake.

Chapter V

The celebration went off well. The friends were all present, both the young and the old. Among the young were Flossie and Gracie Peanut and their brother Adelbert, who was a rising young journeyman tinner, also Hosannah Dilkins, Jr., journeyman plasterer, just out of his apprenticeship. For many months Adelbert and Hosannah had been showing interest in Gwendolen and Clytemnestra Foster, and the parents of the girls had noticed this with private satisfaction. But they suddenly realized now that that feeling had passed. They recognized that the changed financial conditions had raised up a social bar between their daughters and the young mechanics. The daughters could now look higher – and must. Yes, must. They need marry nothing below the grade of lawyer or merchant; poppa and momma would take care of this; there must be no mesalliances.

However, these thinkings and projects of theirs were private, and did not show on the surface, and therefore threw no shadow upon the celebration. What showed upon the surface was a serene and lofty contentment and a dignity of carriage and gravity of deportment which compelled the admiration and likewise the wonder of the company. All noticed it and all commented upon it, but none was able to divine the secret of it. It was a marvel and a mystery. Three several persons remarked, without suspecting what clever shots they were making:

'It's as if they'd come into property.'

That was just it, indeed.

Most mothers would have taken hold of the matrimonial matter in the old regulation way; they would have given the girls a talking to, of a solemn sort and untactful – a lecture calculated to defeat its own purpose, by producing tears and secret rebellion; and the said mothers would have further damaged the business by requesting the young mechanics to discontinue their attentions. But this mother was different. She was practical. She said nothing to any of the young people concerned, nor to anyone else except Sally. He listened to her and understood; understood and admired. He said:

'I get the idea. Instead of finding fault with the samples on view, thus hurting feelings and obstructing trade without occasion, you merely offer a higher class of goods for the money, and leave nature to take her course. It's wisdom, Aleck, solid wisdom, and sound as a nut. Who's your fish? Have you nominated him yet?'

No, she hadn't. They must look the market over – which they did. To start with, they considered and discussed

Brandish, rising young lawyer, and Fulton, rising young dentist. Sally must invite them to dinner. But not right away; there was no hurry, Aleck said. Keep an eye on the pair, and wait; nothing would be lost by going slowly in so important a matter.

It turned out that this was wisdom, too; for inside of three weeks Aleck made a wonderful strike which swelled her imaginary hundred thousand to four hundred thousand of the same quality. She and Sally were in the clouds that evening. For the first time they introduced champagne at dinner. Not real champagne, but plenty real enough for the amount of imagination expended on it. It was Sally that did it, and Aleck weakly submitted. At bottom both were troubled and ashamed, for he was a high-up Son of Temperance, and at funerals wore an apron which no dog could look upon and retain his reason and his opinion; and she was a W. C. T. U., with all that that implies of boiler-iron virtue and unendurable holiness. But there it was; the pride of riches was beginning its disintegrating work. They had lived to prove, once more, a sad truth which had been proven many times before in the world: that whereas principle is a great and noble protection against showy and degrading vanities and vices, poverty is worth six of it. More than four hundred thousand dollars to the good. They took up the matrimonial matter again. Neither the dentist nor the lawyer was mentioned; there was no occasion, they were out of the running. Disqualified. They discussed the son of the pork packer and the son of the village banker. But finally, as in the previous case, they concluded to wait and think, and go cautiously and sure.

Luck came their way again. Aleck, ever watchful saw a great and risky chance, and took a daring flyer. A time of trembling, of doubt, of awful uneasiness followed, for non-success meant absolute ruin and nothing short of it. Then came the result, and Aleck, faint with joy, could hardly control her voice when she said:

'The suspense is over, Sally – and we are worth a cold million!'

Sally wept for gratitude, and said:

'Oh, Electra, jewel of women, darling of my heart, we are free at last, we roll in wealth, we need never scrimp again. It's a case for Veuve Cliquot!' and he got out a pint of spruce beer and made sacrifice, he saying:

'Damn the expense,' and she rebuking him gently with reproachful but humid and happy eyes.

They shelved the pork packer's son and the banker's son, and sat down to consider the Governor's son and the son of the Congressman.

Chapter VI

It were a weariness to follow in detail the leaps and bounds the Foster fictitious finances took from this time forth. It was marvellous, it was dizzying, it was dazzling. Everything Aleck touched turned to fairy gold, and heaped itself glittering toward the firmament. Millions upon millions poured in, and still the mighty stream flowed thundering along, still its vast volume increased. Five millions – ten millions – twenty – thirty – was there never to be an end?

Two years swept by in a splendid delirium, the intoxicated Fosters scarcely noticing the flight of time. They were now worth three hundred million dollars; they were in every board of directors of every prodigious combine in the country; and still as time drifted along, the millions went on piling up, five at a time, ten at a time, as fast as they could tally them off, almost. The three hundred double itself – then doubled again – and yet again – and yet once more.

Twenty-four hundred millions!

The business was getting a little confused. It was necessary to take an account of stock, and straighten it out. The Fosters knew it, they felt it, they realized that it was imperative; but they also knew that to do it properly and perfectly the task must be carried to a finish without a break when once it was begun. A ten-hours' job; and where could *they* find ten leisure hours in a bunch? Sally was selling pins and sugar and calico all day and every day; Aleck was cooking and washing dishes and sweeping and making beds all day and every day, with none to help, for the daughters were being saved up for high society. The Fosters knew there was one way to get the ten hours, and only one. Both were ashamed to name it; each waited for the other to do it. Finally Sally said:

'Somebody's got to give in. It's up to me. Consider that I've named it – never mind pronouncing it out aloud.'

Aleck coloured, but was grateful. Without further remark, they fell. Fell, and – broke the Sabbath. For that was their only free ten-hour stretch. It was but another step in the downward path. Others would follow. Vast wealth has temptations which fatally and surely undermine the moral structure of persons not habituated to its possession.

They pulled down the shades and broke the Sabbath. With hard and patient labour they overhauled their holdings and listed them. And a long-drawn procession of formidable names it was! Starting with the Railway Systems, Steamer Lines, Standard Oil, Ocean Cables, Diluted Telegraph, and all the rest, and winding up with Klondike, De Beers, Tammany Graft, and Shady Privileges in the Post-office Department.

Twenty-four hundred millions, and all safely planted in Good Things, gilt-edged and interest-bearing. Income, $120,000,000 a year. Aleck fetched a long purr of soft delight, and said:

'Is it enough?'

'It is, Aleck.'

'What shall we do?'

'Stand pat.'

'Retire from business?'

'That's it.'

'I am agreed. The good work is finished; we will take a long rest and enjoy the money.'

'Good! Aleck!'

'Yes, dear?'

'How much of the income can we spend?'

'The whole of it.'

It seemed to her husband that a ton of chains fell from his limbs. He did not say a word; he was happy beyond the power of speech.

After that, they broke the Sabbaths right along as fast as they turned up. It is the first wrong step that counts. Every Sunday they put in the whole day, after morning service, on inventions – inventions of ways to spend the money. They got to continuing this delicious dissipation until past midnight; and at every seance Aleck lavished millions upon great charities and religious enterprises, and Sally lavished like sums upon matters to which (at first) he gave definite names. Only at first. Later the names gradually lost sharpness of outline, and eventually faded into 'sundries,' thus becoming entirely – but safely – undescriptive. For Sally was crumbling. The placing of these millions added seriously and most uncomfortably to the family expenses – in tallow candles.

For a while Aleck was worried. Then, after a little, she ceased to worry, for the occasion of it was gone. She was pained, she was grieved, she was ashamed; but she said nothing, and so became an accessory. Sally was taking candles; he was robbing the store. It is ever thus. Vast wealth, to the person unaccustomed to it, is a bane; it eats into the flesh and bone of his morals. When the Fosters were poor, they could have been trusted with untold candles. But now they – but let us not dwell upon it. From candles to apples is but a step: Sally got to taking apples; then soap; then maple sugar; then canned goods; then crockery. How easy it is to go from bad to worse, when once we have started upon a downward course!

Meantime, other effects had been milestoning the course of the Fosters' splendid financial march. The fictitious brick dwelling had given place to an imaginary granite one with a checker-board mansard roof; in time this one disappeared and gave place to a still grander home – and so on and so on. Mansion after mansion, made of air, rose, higher, broader, finer, and each in its turn vanished away; until now in these latter great days, our dreamers were in fancy housed, in a distant region, in a sumptuous vast palace which looked out from a leafy summit upon a noble prospect of vale and river and receding hills steeped in tinted mists – and all private, all the property of the dreamers; a palace swarming with liveried servants, and populous with guests of fame and power, hailing from all the world's capitals, foreign and domestic.

This palace was far, far away toward the rising sun, immeasurably remote, astronomically remote, in Newport, Rhode Island, Holy Land of High Society, ineffable Domain of the American Aristocracy. As a rule they spent a part of every Sabbath – after morning service – in this sumptuous home, the rest of it they spent in Europe, or in dawdling around in their private yacht. Six days of sordid and plodding fact life at home on the ragged edge of Lakeside and straitened means, the seventh in Fairyland – such had been their program and their habit.

In their sternly restricted fact life they remained as of old – plodding, diligent, careful, practical, economical. They stuck loyally to the little Presbyterian Church, and laboured faithfully in its interests and stood by its high and tough doctrines with all their mental and spiritual energies. But in their dream life they obeyed the invitations of their fancies, whatever they might be, and howsoever the fancies might change. Aleck's fancies were not very capricious, and not frequent, but Sally's scattered a good deal. Aleck, in her dream life, went over to the Episcopal camp, on account of its large official titles; next she became High church on account of the candles and shows; and next she naturally changed to Rome, where there were cardinals and more candles. But these excursions were nothing to Sally's. His dream life was a glowing and continuous and persistent excitement, and he kept every part of it fresh and sparkling by frequent changes, the religious part along with the rest. He worked his religions hard, and changed them with his shirt.

The liberal spendings of the Fosters upon their fancies began early in their prosperities, and grew in prodigality step by step with their advancing fortunes. In time they became truly enormous. Aleck built a university or two per Sunday; also a hospital or two; also a Rowton hotel or so; also a batch of churches; now and then a cathedral; and once, with untimely and ill-chosen playfulness, Sally said,

'It was a cold day when she didn't ship a cargo of missionaries to persuade unreflecting Chinamen to trade off twenty-four carat Confucianism for counterfeit Christianity.'

This rude and unfeeling language hurt Aleck to the heart, and she went from the presence crying. That spectacle went to his own heart, and in his pain and shame he would have given worlds to have those unkind words back. She had uttered no syllable of reproach – and that cut him. Not one suggestion that he look at his own record – and she could have made, oh, so many, and such blistering ones! Her generous silence brought a swift revenge, for it turned his thoughts upon himself, it summoned before him a spectral procession, a moving vision of his life as he had been leading it these past few years of limitless prosperity, and as he sat there reviewing it his cheeks burned and his soul was steeped in humiliation. Look at her life – how fair it was, and tending ever upward; and look at his own – how frivolous, how charged with mean vanities, how selfish, how empty, how ignoble! And its trend – never upward, but downward, ever downward!

He instituted comparisons between her record and his own. He had found fault with her – so he mused – *he*! And what could he say for himself? When she built her first church what was he doing? Gathering other blasé multimillionaires into a Poker Club; defiling his own palace with it; losing hundreds of thousands to it at every sitting, and sillily vain of the admiring notoriety it made for him. When she was building her first university, what was he doing? Polluting himself with a gay and dissipated secret life in the company of other fast bloods, multimillionaires in money and paupers in character. When she was building her first foundling asylum, what was he doing? Alas! When she was projecting her noble Society for the Purifying of the Sex, what was he doing? Ah, what, indeed! When she and the W. C. T. U. and the Woman with the Hatchet, moving with resistless march, were sweeping the fatal bottle from the land, what was he doing? Getting drunk three times a day. When she, builder of a hundred cathedrals, was being gratefully welcomed and blest in papal Rome and decorated with the Golden Rose which she had so honourably earned, what was he doing? Breaking the bank at Monte Carlo.

He stopped. He could go no farther; he could not bear the rest. He rose up, with a great resolution upon his lips:

this secret life should be revealed, and confessed; no longer would he live it clandestinely, he would go and tell her All.

And that is what he did. He told her All; and wept upon her bosom; wept, and moaned, and begged for her forgiveness. It was a profound shock, and she staggered under the blow, but he was her own, the core of her heart, the blessing of her eyes, her all in all, she could deny him nothing, and she forgave him. She felt that he could never again be quite to her what he had been before; she knew that he could only repent, and not reform; yet all morally defaced and decayed as he was, was he not her own, her very own, the idol of her deathless worship? She said she was his serf, his slave, and she opened her yearning heart and took him in.

Chapter VII

One Sunday afternoon sometime after this they were sailing the summer seas in their dream yacht, and reclining in lazy luxury under the awning of the after-deck. There was silence, for each was busy with his own thoughts. These seasons of silence had insensibly been growing more and more frequent of late; the old nearness and cordiality were waning. Sally's terrible revelation had done its work; Aleck had tried hard to drive the memory of it out of her mind, but it would not go, and the shame and bitterness of it were poisoning her gracious dream life. She could see now (on Sundays) that her husband was becoming a bloated and repulsive Thing. She could not close her eyes to this, and in these days she no longer looked at him, Sundays, when she could help it.

But she – was she herself without blemish? Alas, she knew she was not. She was keeping a secret from him, she was acting dishonourably toward him, and many a pang it was costing her. *She was breaking the compact, and concealing it from him.* Under strong temptation she had gone into business again; she had risked their whole fortune in a purchase of all the railway systems and coal and steel companies in the country on a margin, and she was now trembling, every Sabbath hour, lest through some chance word of hers he find it out. In her misery and remorse for this treachery she could not keep her heart from going out to him in pity; she was filled with compunctions to see him lying there, drunk and contented, and never suspecting. Never suspecting – trusting her with a perfect and pathetic trust, and she holding over him by a thread a possible calamity of so devastating a –

'*Say* – Aleck?'

The interrupting words brought her suddenly to herself. She was grateful to have that persecuting subject from her thoughts, and she answered, with much of the old-time tenderness in her tone:

'Yes, dear.'

'Do you know, Aleck, I think we are making a mistake – that is, you are. I mean about the marriage business.'

He sat up, fat and froggy and benevolent, like a bronze Buddha, and grew earnest.

'Consider – it's more than five years. You've continued the same policy from the start: with every rise, always holding on for five points higher. Always when I think we are going to have some weddings, you see a bigger thing ahead, and I undergo another disappointment. *I* think you are too hard to please. Someday we'll get left. First, we turned down the dentist and the lawyer. That was all right – it was sound. Next, we turned down the banker's son and the pork-butcher's heir – right again, and sound. Next, we turned down the Congressman's son and the Governor's – right as a trivet, I confess it. Next the Senator's son and the son of the Vice-President of the United States – perfectly right, there's no permanency about those little distinctions. Then you went for the aristocracy; and I thought we had struck oil at last – yes. We would make a plunge at the Four Hundred, and pull in some ancient lineage, venerable, holy, ineffable, mellow with the antiquity of a hundred and fifty years, disinfected of the ancestral odours of salt-cod and pelts all of a century ago, and unsmirched by a day's work since, and then! Why, then the marriages, of course. But no, along comes a pair of real aristocrats from Europe, and straightway you throw over the half-breeds. It was awfully discouraging, Aleck! Since then, what a procession! You turned down the baronets for a pair of barons; you turned down the barons for a pair of viscounts; the viscounts for a pair of earls; the earls for a pair of marquises; the marquises for a brace of dukes. *Now*, Aleck, cash in! – you've played the limit. You've got a job lot of four dukes under the hammer; of four nationalities; all sound in the wind and limb and pedigree, all bankrupt and in debt up to the ears. They come high, but we can afford it. Come, Aleck, don't delay any longer, don't keep up the suspense: take the whole layout, and leave the girls to choose!'

Aleck had been smiling blandly and contentedly all through this arraignment of her marriage policy, a pleasant light, as of triumph with perhaps a nice surprise peeping out through it, rose in her eyes, and she said, as calmly as she could:

'Sally, what would you say to – *royalty*?'

Prodigious! Poor man, it knocked him silly, and he fell over the garboard strake and barked his shin on the cat-heads. He was dizzy for a moment, then he gathered himself up and limped over and sat down by his wife and beamed his old-time admiration and affection upon her in floods, out of his bleary eyes.

'By George!' he said, fervently, 'Aleck, you *are* great – the greatest woman in the whole earth! I can't ever learn the whole size of you. I can't ever learn the immeasurable deeps of you. Here I've been considering myself qualified to criticize your game. *I!* Why, if I had stopped to think, I'd have known you had a lone hand up your sleeve. Now, dear heart, I'm all red-hot impatience – tell me about it!'

The flattered and happy woman put her lips to his ear and whispered a princely name. It made him catch his breath, it lit his face with exultation.

'Land!' he said, 'it's a stunning catch! He's got a gambling hall, and a graveyard, and a bishop, and a cathedral – all his very own. And all gilt-edged five-hundred-per-cent. stock, every detail of it; the tidiest little property in Europe; and that graveyard – it's the selectest in the world: none but suicides admitted; *yes*, sir, and the free list suspended, too, *all* the time. There isn't much land in the principality, but there's enough: eight hundred acres in the graveyard and forty-two outside. It's a *sovereignty* – that's the main thing; *land's* nothing. There's plenty land, Sahara's drugged with it.'

Aleck glowed; she was profoundly happy. She said:

'Think of it, Sally – it is a family that has never married outside the Royal and Imperial Houses of Europe: our grandchildren will sit upon thrones!'

'True as you live, Aleck – and bear sceptres, too; and handle them as naturally and nonchalantly as I handle a yardstick. It's a grand catch, Aleck. He's corralled, is he? Can't get away? You didn't take him on a margin?'

'No. Trust me for that. He's not a liability, he's an asset. So is the other one.'

'Who is it, Aleck?'

'His Royal Highness Sigismund-Siegfried-Lauenfeld-Dinkelspiel-Schwartzenberg Blutwurst, Hereditary Grand Duke of Katzenyammer.'

'No! You can't mean it!'

'It's as true as I'm sitting here, I give you my word,' she answered.

His cup was full, and he hugged her to his heart with rapture, saying:

'How wonderful it all seems, and how beautiful! It's one of the oldest and noblest of the three hundred and sixty-four ancient German principalities, and one of the few that was allowed to retain its royal estate when Bismarck got done trimming them. I know that farm, I've been there. It's got a ropewalk and a candle factory and an army. Standing army.

Infantry and cavalry. Three soldiers and a horse. Aleck, it's been a long wait, and full of heartbreak and hope deferred, but God knows I am happy now. Happy, and grateful to you, my own, who have done it all. When is it to be?'

'Next Sunday.'

'Good. And we'll want to do these weddings up in the very regalest style that's going. It's properly due to the royal quality of the parties of the first part. Now as I understand it, there is only one kind of marriage that is sacred to royalty, exclusive to royalty: it's the morganatic.'

'What do they call it that for, Sally?'

'I don't know; but anyway it's royal, and royal only.'

'Then we will insist upon it. More – I will compel it. It is morganatic marriage or none.'

'That settles it!' said Sally, rubbing his hands with delight.

'And it will be the very first in America. Aleck, it will make Newport sick.'

Then they fell silent, and drifted away upon their dream wings to the far regions of the earth to invite all the crowned heads and their families and provide gratis transportation to them.

Chapter VIII

During three days the couple walked upon air, with their heads in the clouds. They were but vaguely conscious of their surroundings; they saw all things dimly, as through a veil; they were steeped in dreams, often they did not hear when they were spoken to; they often did not understand when they heard; they answered confusedly or at random; Sally sold molasses by weight, sugar by the yard, and furnished soap when asked for candles, and Aleck put the cat in the wash and fed milk to the soiled linen. Everybody was stunned and amazed, and went about muttering,

'What *can* be the matter with the Fosters?'

Three days. Then came events! Things had taken a happy turn, and for forty-eight hours Aleck's imaginary corner had been booming. Up – up – still up! Cost point was passed. Still up – and up – and up! Five points above cost – then ten – fifteen – twenty! Twenty points cold profit on the vast venture, now, and Aleck's imaginary brokers were shouting frantically by imaginary long-distance,

'Sell! sell! for Heaven's sake *sell*!'

She broke the splendid news to Sally, and he, too, said,

'Sell! Sell – oh, don't make a blunder, now, you own the earth! – sell, sell!'

But she set her iron will and lashed it amidships, and said she would hold on for five points more if she died for it.

It was a fatal resolve. The very next day came the historic crash, the record crash, the devastating crash, when the bottom fell out of Wall Street, and the whole body of gilt-edged stocks dropped ninety-five points in five hours, and the multimillionaire was seen begging his bread in the Bowery. Aleck sternly held her grip and 'put up' as long as she could, but at last there came a call which she was powerless to meet, and her imaginary brokers sold her out. Then, and not till then, the man in her was vanished, and the woman in her resumed sway. She put her arms about her husband's neck and wept, saying:

'I am to blame, do not forgive me, I cannot bear it. We are paupers! Paupers, and I am so miserable. The weddings will never come off; all that is past; we could not even buy the dentist, now.'

A bitter reproach was on Sally's tongue:

'I *begged* you to sell, but you.'

He did not say it; he had not the heart to add a hurt to that broken and repentant spirit. A nobler thought came to him and he said:

'Bear up, my Aleck, all is not lost! You really never invested a penny of my uncle's bequest, but only its unmaterialized future; what we have lost was only the incremented harvest from that future by your incomparable financial judgment and sagacity. Cheer up, banish these griefs; we still have the thirty thousand untouched; and with the experience which you have acquired, think what you will be able to do with it in a couple years! The marriages are not off, they are only postponed.'

These were blessed words. Aleck saw how true they were, and their influence was electric; her tears ceased to flow, and her great spirit rose to its full stature again. With flashing eye and grateful heart, and with hand uplifted in pledge and prophecy, she said:

'Now and here I proclaim… '

But she was interrupted by a visitor. It was the editor and proprietor of the *Sagamore*. He had happened into Lakeside to pay a duty call upon an obscure grandmother of his who was nearing the end of her pilgrimage, and with the idea of combining business with grief he had looked up the Fosters, who had been so absorbed in other things for the past four years that they neglected to pay up their subscription. Six dollars due. No visitor could have been more welcome. He would know all about Uncle Tilbury and what his chances might be getting to be, cemeterywards. They could, of course, ask no questions, for that would squelch the bequest, but they could nibble around on the edge of the subject and hope for results. The scheme did not work. The obtuse editor did not know he was being nibbled at; but at last, chance accomplished what art had failed in. In illustration of something under discussion which required the help of metaphor, the editor said:

'Land, it's as tough as Tilbury Foster! – as *we* say.'

It was sudden, and it made the Fosters jump. The editor noticed, and said, apologetically:

'No harm intended, I assure you. It's just a saying; just a joke, you know – nothing in it. Relation of yours?'

Sally crowded his burning eagerness down, and answered with all the indifference he could assume:

'I – well, not that I know of, but we've heard of him.'

The editor was thankful, and resumed his composure. Sally added:

'Is he – is he – well?'

'Is he *well*? Why, bless you he's in Sheol these five years!'

The Fosters were trembling with grief, though it felt like joy. Sally said, non-committally – and tentatively:

'Ah, well, such is life, and none can escape – not even the rich are spared.'

The editor laughed.

'If you are including Tilbury,' said he, 'it don't apply. *He* hadn't a cent; the town had to bury him.'

The Fosters sat petrified for two minutes; petrified and cold. Then, white-faced and weak-voiced, Sally asked:

'Is it true? Do you *know* it to be true?'

'Well, I should say! I was one of the executors. He hadn't anything to leave but a wheelbarrow, and he left that to me. It hadn't any wheel, and wasn't any good. Still, it was something, and so, to square up, I scribbled off a sort of a little obituarial send-off for him, but it got crowded out.'

The Fosters were not listening – their cup was full, it could contain no more. They sat with bowed heads, dead to all things but the ache at their hearts.

An hour later. Still they sat there, bowed, motionless, silent, the visitor long ago gone, they unaware.

Then they stirred, and lifted their heads wearily, and gazed at each other wistfully, dreamily, dazed; then presently began to twaddle to each other in a wandering and childish way. At intervals they lapsed into silences, leaving a sentence unfinished, seemingly either unaware of it or losing their way. Sometimes, when they woke out of these silences they had a dim and transient consciousness that something had happened to their minds; then with a dumb and yearning solicitude they would softly caress each other's hands in mutual compassion and support, as if they would say:

'I am near you, I will not forsake you, we will bear it together; somewhere there is release and forgetfulness, somewhere there is a grave and peace; be patient, it will not be long.'

They lived yet two years, in mental night, always brooding, steeped in vague regrets and melancholy dreams, never speaking; then release came to both on the same day.

Toward the end the darkness lifted from Sally's ruined mind for a moment, and he said:

'Vast wealth, acquired by sudden and unwholesome means, is a snare. It did us no good, transient were its feverish pleasures; yet for its sake we threw away our sweet and simple and happy life – let others take warning by us.'

He lay silent awhile, with closed eyes; then as the chill of death crept upward toward his heart, and consciousness was fading from his brain, he muttered:

'Money had brought him misery, and he took his revenge upon us, who had done him no harm. He had his desire: with base and cunning calculation he left us but thirty thousand, knowing we would try to increase it, and ruin our life and break our hearts. Without added expense he could have left us far above desire of increase, far above the temptation to speculate, and a kinder soul would have done it; but in him was no generous spirit, no pity, no.'

The Parasite

Chapter I

March 24. The spring is fairly with us now. Outside my laboratory window the great chestnut tree is all covered with the big, glutinous, gummy buds, some of which have already begun to break into little green shuttlecocks. As you walk down the lanes you are conscious of the rich, silent forces of nature working all around you. The wet earth smells fruitful and luscious. Green shoots are peeping out everywhere. The twigs are stiff with their sap; and the moist, heavy English air is laden with a faintly resinous perfume. Buds in the hedges, lambs beneath them everywhere the work of reproduction going forward!

I can see it without, and I can feel it within. We also have our spring when the little arterioles dilate, the lymph flows in a brisker stream, the glands work harder, winnowing and straining. Every year nature readjusts the whole machine. I can feel the ferment in my blood at this very moment, and as the cool sunshine pours through my window I could dance about in it like a gnat. So I should, only that Charles Sadler would rush upstairs to know what was the matter. Besides, I must remember that I am Professor Gilroy. An old professor may afford to be natural, but when fortune has given one of the first chairs in the university to a man of four-and-thirty he must try and act the part consistently.

What a fellow Wilson is! If I could only throw the same enthusiasm into physiology that he does into psychology, I should become a Claude Bernard at the least. His whole life and soul and energy work to one end. He drops to sleep collating his results of the past day, and he wakes to plan his researches for the coming one. And yet, outside the narrow circle who follow his proceedings, he gets so little credit for it. Physiology is a recognized science. If I add even a brick to the edifice, everyone sees and applauds it. But Wilson is trying to dig the foundations for a science of the future. His work is underground and does not show. Yet he goes on uncomplainingly, corresponding with a hundred semi-maniacs in the hope of finding one reliable witness, sifting a hundred lies on the chance of gaining one little speck of truth, collating old books, devouring new ones, experimenting, lecturing, trying to light up in others the fiery interest which is consuming him. I am filled with wonder and admiration when I think of him, and yet, when he asks me to associate myself with his researches, I am compelled to tell him that, in their present state, they offer little attraction to a man who is devoted to exact science. If he could show me something positive and objective, I might then be tempted to approach the question from its physiological side. So long as half his subjects are tainted with charlatanerie and the other half with hysteria we physiologists must content ourselves with the body and leave the mind to our descendants.

No doubt I am a materialist. Agatha says that I am a rank one. I tell her that is an excellent reason for shortening our engagement, since I am in such urgent need of her spirituality. And yet I may claim to be a curious example of the effect of education upon temperament, for by nature I am, unless I deceive myself, a highly psychic man. I was a nervous, sensitive boy, a dreamer, a somnambulist, full of impressions and intuitions. My black hair, my dark eyes, my thin, olive face, my tapering fingers, are all characteristic of my real temperament, and cause experts like Wilson to claim me as their own. But my brain is soaked with exact knowledge. I have trained myself to deal only with fact and with proof. Surmise and fancy have no place in my scheme of thought. Show me what I can see with my microscope, cut with my scalpel, weigh in my balance, and I will devote a lifetime to its investigation. But when you ask me to study feelings, impressions, suggestions, you ask me to do what is distasteful and even demoralizing. A departure from pure reason affects me like an evil smell or a musical discord.

Which is a very sufficient reason why I am a little loath to go to Professor Wilson's tonight. Still I feel that I could hardly get out of the invitation without positive rudeness; and, now that Mrs. Marden and Agatha are going, of course I would not if I could. But I had rather meet them anywhere else. I know that Wilson would draw me into this nebulous semi-science of his if he could. In his enthusiasm he is perfectly impervious to hints or remonstrances. Nothing short of a positive quarrel will make him realize my aversion to the whole business. I have no doubt that he has some new mesmerist or clairvoyant or medium or trickster of some sort whom he is going to exhibit to us, for even his entertainments bear upon his hobby. Well, it will be a treat for Agatha, at any rate. She is interested in it, as woman usually is in whatever is vague and mystical and indefinite.

10.50 P. M. This diary-keeping of mine is, I fancy, the outcome of that scientific habit of mind about which I wrote this morning. I like to register impressions while they are fresh. Once a day at least I endeavour to define my own mental position. It is a useful piece of self-analysis, and has, I fancy, a steadying effect upon the character. Frankly, I must confess that my own needs what stiffening I can give it. I fear that, after all, much of my neurotic temperament survives, and that I am far from that cool, calm precision which characterizes Murdoch or Pratt-Haldane. Otherwise, why should the tomfoolery which I have witnessed this evening have set my nerves thrilling so that even now I am all unstrung? My only comfort is that neither Wilson nor Miss Penclosa nor even Agatha could have possibly known my weakness.

And what in the world was there to excite me? Nothing, or so little that it will seem ludicrous when I set it down.

The Mardens got to Wilson's before me. In fact, I was one of the last to arrive and found the room crowded. I had hardly time to say a word to Mrs Marden and to Agatha, who was looking charming in white and pink, with glittering wheat ears in her hair, when Wilson came twitching at my sleeve.

'You want something positive, Gilroy,' said he, drawing me apart into a corner. 'My dear fellow, I have a phenomenon a phenomenon!'

I should have been more impressed had I not heard the same before. His sanguine spirit turns every firefly into a star.

'No possible question about the bona fides this time,' said he, in answer, perhaps, to some little gleam of amusement in my eyes.

'My wife has known her for many years. They both come from Trinidad, you know. Miss Penclosa has only been in England a month or two, and knows no one outside the university circle, but I assure you that the things she has told us suffice in themselves to establish clairvoyance upon an absolutely scientific basis. There is nothing like her, amateur or professional. Come and be introduced!'

I like none of these mystery-mongers, but the amateur least of all. With the paid performer you may pounce upon him and expose him the instant that you have seen through his trick. He is there to deceive you, and you are there to find him out. But what are you to do with the friend of your host's wife? Are you to turn on a light suddenly and expose her slapping a surreptitious banjo? Or are you to hurl cochineal over her evening frock when she steals around with her phosphorus bottle and her supernatural platitude? There would be a scene, and you would be looked upon as a brute. So you have your choice of being that or a dupe. I was in no very good humour as I followed Wilson to the lady.

Anyone less like my idea of a West Indian could not be imagined. She was a small, frail creature, well over forty, I should say, with a pale, peaky face, and hair of a very light shade of chestnut. Her presence was insignificant and her manner retiring. In any group of ten women she would have been the last whom one would have picked out. Her eyes were perhaps her most remarkable, and also, I am compelled to say, her least pleasant, feature. They were grey in colour, grey with a shade of green, and their expression struck me as being decidedly furtive. I wonder if furtive is the word, or should I have said fierce? On second thoughts, feline would have expressed it better. A crutch leaning against the wall told me what was painfully evident when she rose: that one of her legs was crippled.

So I was introduced to Miss Penclosa, and it did not escape me that as my name was mentioned she glanced across at Agatha. Wilson had evidently been talking. And presently, no doubt, thought I, she will inform me by occult means that I am engaged to a young lady with wheat ears in her hair. I wondered how much more Wilson had been telling her about me.

'Professor Gilroy is a terrible sceptic,' said he; 'I hope, Miss Penclosa, that you will be able to convert him.'

She looked keenly up at me.

'Professor Gilroy is quite right to be sceptical if he has not seen anything convincing,' said she.

'I should have thought,' she added, 'that you would yourself have been an excellent subject.'

'For what, may I ask?' said I.

'Well, for mesmerism, for example.'

'My experience has been that mesmerists go for their subjects to those who are mentally unsound. All their results are vitiated, as it seems to me, by the fact that they are dealing with abnormal organisms.'

'Which of these ladies would you say possessed a normal organism?' she asked.

'I should like you to select the one who seems to you to have the best-balanced mind. Should we say the girl in pink and white? Miss Agatha Marden, I think the name is.'

'Yes, I should attach weight to any results from her.'

'I have never tried how far she is impressionable. Of course some people respond much more rapidly than others. May I ask how far your scepticism extends? I suppose that you admit the mesmeric sleep and the power of suggestion.'

'I admit nothing, Miss Penclosa.'

'Dear me, I thought science had got further than that. Of course I know nothing about the scientific side of it. I only know what I can do. You see the girl in red, for example, over near the Japanese jar. I shall will that she come across to us.'

She bent forward as she spoke and dropped her fan upon the floor. The girl whisked round and came straight toward us, with an enquiring look upon her face, as if someone had called her.

'What do you think of that, Gilroy?' cried Wilson, in a kind of ecstasy.

I did not dare to tell him what I thought of it. To me it was the most barefaced, shameless piece of imposture that I had ever witnessed. The collusion and the signal had really been too obvious.

'Professor Gilroy is not satisfied,' said she, glancing up at me with her strange little eyes.

'My poor fan is to get the credit of that experiment. Well, we must try something else. Miss Marden, would you have any objection to my putting you off?'

'Oh, I should love it!' cried Agatha.

By this time all the company had gathered around us in a circle, the shirt-fronted men, and the white-throated women, some awed, some critical, as though it were something between a religious ceremony and a conjurer's entertainment. A red velvet armchair had been pushed into the centre, and Agatha lay back in it, a little flushed and trembling slightly from excitement. I could see it from the vibration of the wheat ears. Miss Penclosa rose from her seat and stood over her, leaning upon her crutch.

And there was a change in the woman. She no longer seemed small or insignificant. Twenty years were gone from her age. Her eyes were shining, a tinge of colour had come into her sallow cheeks, her whole figure had expanded. So I have seen a dull-eyed, listless lad change in an instant into briskness and life when given a task of which he felt himself master. She looked down at Agatha with an expression which I resented from the bottom of my soul, the expression with which a Roman empress might have looked at her kneeling slave. Then with a quick, commanding gesture she tossed up her arms and swept them slowly down in front of her.

I was watching Agatha narrowly. During three passes she seemed to be simply amused. At the fourth I observed a slight glazing of her eyes, accompanied by some dilation of her pupils. At the sixth there was a momentary rigour. At the seventh her lids began to droop. At the tenth her eyes were closed, and her breathing was slower and fuller than usual. I tried as I watched to preserve my scientific calm, but a foolish, causeless agitation convulsed me. I trust that I hid it, but I felt as a child feels in the dark. I could not have believed that I was still open to such weakness.

'She is in the trance,' said Miss Penclosa.

'She is sleeping!' I cried.

'Wake her, then!'

I pulled her by the arm and shouted in her ear. She might have been dead for all the impression that I could make. Her body was there on the velvet chair. Her organs were acting her heart, her lungs. But her soul! It had slipped from beyond our ken. Whither had it gone? What power had dispossessed it? I was puzzled and disconcerted.

'So much for the mesmeric sleep,' said Miss Penclosa.

'As regards suggestion, whatever I may suggest Miss Marden will infallibly do, whether it be now or after she has awakened from her trance. Do you demand proof of it?'

'Certainly,' said I.

'You shall have it.' I saw a smile pass over her face, as though an amusing thought had struck her. She stooped and whispered earnestly into her subject's ear. Agatha, who had been so deaf to me, nodded her head as she listened.

'Awake!' cried Miss Penclosa, with a sharp tap of her crutch upon the floor. The eyes opened, the glazing cleared slowly away, and the soul looked out once more after its strange eclipse.

We went away early. Agatha was none the worse for her strange excursion, but I was nervous and unstrung, unable to listen to or answer the stream of comments which Wilson was pouring out for my benefit. As I bade her goodnight Miss Penclosa slipped a piece of paper into my hand.

'Pray forgive me,' said she, 'if I take means to overcome your scepticism. Open this note at ten o'clock tomorrow morning. It is a little private test.'

I can't imagine what she means, but there is the note, and it shall be opened as she directs. My head is aching, and I have written enough for tonight. Tomorrow I dare say that what seems so inexplicable will take quite another complexion. I shall not surrender my convictions without a struggle.

March 25. I am amazed, confounded. It is clear that I must reconsider my opinion upon this matter. But first let me place on record what has occurred.

I had finished breakfast, and was looking over some diagrams with which my lecture is to be illustrated, when my housekeeper entered to tell me that Agatha was in my study and wished to see me immediately. I glanced at the clock and saw with sunrise that it was only half-past nine.

When I entered the room, she was standing on the hearth rug facing me. Something in her pose chilled me and checked the words which were rising to my lips. Her veil was half down, but I could see that she was pale and that her expression was constrained.

'Austin,' she said, 'I have come to tell you that our engagement is at an end.'

I staggered. I believe that I literally did stagger. I know that I found myself leaning against the bookcase for support.

'But but… ' I stammered. 'This is very sudden, Agatha.'

'Yes, Austin, I have come here to tell you that our engagement is at an end.'

'But surely,' I cried, 'you will give me some reason! This is unlike you, Agatha. Tell me how I have been unfortunate enough to offend you.'

'It is all over, Austin.'

'But why? You must be under some delusion, Agatha. Perhaps you have been told some falsehood about me. Or you may have misunderstood something that I have said to you. Only let me know what it is, and a word may set it all right.'

'We must consider it all at an end.'

'But you left me last night without a hint at any disagreement. What could have occurred in the interval to change you so? It must have been something that happened last night. You have been thinking it over and you have disapproved of my conduct. Was it the mesmerism? Did you blame me for letting that woman exercise her power over you? You know that at the least sign I should have interfered.'

'It is useless, Austin. All is over:'

Her voice was cold and measured; her manner strangely formal and hard. It seemed to me that she was absolutely resolved not to be drawn into any argument or explanation. As for me, I was shaking with agitation, and I turned my face aside, so ashamed was I that she should see my want of control.

'You must know what this means to me!' I cried. 'It is the blasting of all my hopes and the ruin of my life! You surely will not inflict such a punishment upon me unheard. You will let me know what is the matter. Consider how impossible it would be for me, under any circumstances, to treat you so. For God's sake, Agatha, let me know what I have done!'

She walked past me without a word and opened the door.

'It is quite useless, Austin,' said she. 'You must consider our engagement at an end.'

An instant later she was gone, and, before I could recover myself sufficiently to follow her, I heard the hall-door close behind her.

I rushed into my room to change my coat, with the idea of hurrying round to Mrs. Marden's to learn from her what the cause of my misfortune might be. So shaken was I that I could hardly lace my boots. Never shall I forget those horrible ten minutes. I had just pulled on my overcoat when the clock upon the mantelpiece struck ten.

Ten! I associated the idea with Miss Penclosa's note. It was lying before me on the table, and I tore it open. It was scribbled in pencil in a peculiarly angular handwriting.

'MY DEAR PROFESSOR GILROY [it said]: Pray excuse the personal nature of the test which I am giving you. Professor Wilson happened to mention the relations between you and my subject of this evening, and it struck me that nothing could be more convincing to you than if I were to suggest to Miss Marden that she should call upon you at half-past nine tomorrow morning and suspend your engagement for half an hour or so. Science is so exacting that it is difficult to give a satisfying test, but I am convinced that this at least will be an action which she would be most unlikely to do of her own free will. Forget anything that she may have said, as she has really nothing whatever to do with it, and will certainly not recollect anything about it. I write this note to shorten your anxiety, and to beg you to forgive me for the momentary unhappiness which my suggestion must have caused you.

'Yours faithfully;
'HELEN PENCLOSA.

Really, when I had read the note, I was too relieved to be angry. It was a liberty. Certainly it was a very great liberty indeed on the part of a lady whom I had only met once. But, after all, I had challenged her by my scepticism. It may have been, as she said, a little difficult to devise a test which would satisfy me.

And she had done that. There could be no question at all upon the point. For me hypnotic suggestion was finally established. It took its place from now onward as one of the facts of life. That Agatha, who of all women of my acquaintance has the best-balanced mind, had been reduced to a condition of automatism appeared to be certain. A person at a distance had worked her as an engineer on the shore might guide a Brennan torpedo. A second soul had stepped in, as it were, had pushed her own aside, and had seized her nervous mechanism, saying:

'I will work this for half an hour.'

And Agatha must have been unconscious as she came and as she returned. Could she make her way in safety through the streets in such a state? I put on my hat and hurried around to see if all was well with her.

Yes. She was at home. I was shown into the drawing room and found her sitting with a book upon her lap.

'You are an early visitor, Austin,' said she, smiling.

'And you have been an even earlier one,' I answered.

She looked puzzled.

'What do you mean?' she asked.

'You have not been out today?'

'No, certainly not.'

'Agatha,' said I seriously, 'would you mind telling me exactly what you have done this morning?'

She laughed at my earnestness.

'You've got on your professional look, Austin. See what comes of being engaged to a man of science. However, I will tell you, though I can't imagine what you want to know for. I got up at eight. I breakfasted at half past. I came into this room at ten minutes past nine and began to read *The Memoirs of Mme. de Rémusat*.

'In a few minutes I did the French lady the bad compliment of dropping to sleep over her pages, and I did you, sir, the very flattering one of dreaming about you. It is only a few minutes since I woke up.'

'And found yourself where you had been before?'

'Why, where else should I find myself?'

'Would you mind telling me, Agatha, what it was that you dreamed about me? It really is not mere curiosity on my part.'

'I merely had a vague impression that you came into it. I cannot recall anything definite.'

'If you have not been out today, Agatha, how is it that your shoes are dusty?'

A pained look came over her face.

'Really, Austin, I do not know what is the matter with you this morning. One would almost think that you doubted my word. If my boots are dusty, it must be, of course, that I have put on a pair which the maid had not cleaned.'

It was perfectly evident that she knew nothing whatever about the matter, and I reflected that, after all, perhaps it was better that I should not enlighten her. It might frighten her, and could serve no good purpose that I could see. I said no more about it, therefore, and left shortly afterwards to give my lecture.

But I am immensely impressed. My horizon of scientific possibilities has suddenly been enormously extended. I no longer wonder at Wilson's demonic energy and enthusiasm. Who would not work hard who had a vast virgin field ready to his hand? Why, I have known the novel shape of a nucleolus, or a trifling peculiarity of striped muscular fibre seen under a 300-diameter lens, fill me with exultation. How petty do such researches seem when compared with this one which strikes at the very roots of life and the nature of the soul! I had always looked upon spirit as a product of matter. The brain, I thought, secreted the mind, as the liver does the bile. But how can this be when I see mind working from a distance and playing upon matter as a musician might upon a violin? The body does not give rise to the soul, then, but is rather the rough instrument by which the spirit manifests itself. The windmill does not give rise to the wind, but only indicates it. It was opposed to my whole habit of thought, and yet it was undeniably possible and worthy of investigation.

And why should I not investigate it? I see that under yesterday's date I said:

'If I could see something positive and objective, I might be tempted to approach it from the physiological aspect.'

Well, I have got my test. I shall be as good as my word. The investigation would, I am sure, be of immense interest. Some of my colleagues might look askance at it, for science is full of unreasoning prejudices, but if Wilson has the courage of his convictions, I can afford to have it also. I shall go to him tomorrow morning to him and to Miss Penclosa. If she can show us so much, it is probable that she can show us more.

Chapter II

March 26. Wilson was, as I had anticipated, very exultant over my conversion, and Miss Penclosa was also demurely pleased at the result of her experiment. Strange what a silent, colourless creature she is save only when she exercises her power! Even talking about it gives her colour and life. She seems to take a singular interest in me. I cannot help observing how her eyes follow me about the room.

We had the most interesting conversation about her own powers. It is just as well to put her views on record, though they cannot, of course, claim any scientific weight.

'You are on the very fringe of the subject,' said she, when I had expressed wonder at the remarkable instance of suggestion which she had shown me.

'I had no direct influence upon Miss Marden when she came round to you. I was not even thinking of her that morning. What I did was to set her mind as I might set the alarm of a clock so that at the hour named it would go off of its own accord. If six months instead of twelve hours had been suggested, it would have been the same.'

'And if the suggestion had been to assassinate me?'

'She would most inevitably have done so.'

'But this is a terrible power!' I cried.

'It is, as you say, a terrible power,' she answered gravely, 'and the more you know of it the more terrible will it seem to you.'

'May I ask,' said I, 'what you meant when you said that this matter of suggestion is only at the fringe of it? What do you consider the essential?'

'I had rather not tell you.'

I was surprised at the decision of her answer.

'You understand,' said I, 'that it is not out of curiosity I ask, but in the hope that I may find some scientific explanation for the facts with which you furnish me.'

'Frankly, Professor Gilroy,' said she, 'I am not at all interested in science, nor do I care whether it can or cannot classify these powers.'

'But I was hoping – '

'Ah, that is quite another thing. If you make it a personal matter,' said she, with the pleasantest of smiles, 'I shall be only too happy to tell you anything you wish to know. Let me see; what was it you asked me? Oh, about the further powers. Professor Wilson won't believe in them, but they are quite true all the same. For example, it is possible for an operator to gain complete command over his subject presuming that the latter is a good one. Without any previous suggestion he may make him do whatever he likes.'

'Without the subject's knowledge?'

'That depends. If the force were strongly exerted, he would know no more about it than Miss Marden did when she came round and frightened you so. Or, if the influence was less powerful, he might be conscious of what he was doing, but be quite unable to prevent himself from doing it.'

'Would he have lost his own willpower, then?'

'It would be overridden by another stronger one.'

'Have you ever exercised this power yourself?'

'Several times.'

'Is your own will so strong, then?'

'Well, it does not entirely depend upon that. Many have strong wills which are not detachable from themselves. The thing is to have the gift of projecting it into another person and superseding his own. I find that the power varies with my own strength and health.'

'Practically, you send your soul into another person's body.'

'Well, you might put it that way.'

'And what does your own body do?'

'It merely feels lethargic.'

'Well, but is there no danger to your own health?' I asked.

'There might be a little. You have to be careful never to let your own consciousness absolutely go; otherwise, you might experience some difficulty in finding your way back again. You must always preserve the connection, as it were. I am afraid I express myself very badly, Professor Gilroy, but of course I don't know how to put these things in a scientific way. I am just giving you my own experiences and my own explanations.'

Well, I read this over now at my leisure, and I marvel at myself! Is this Austin Gilroy, the man who has won his way to the front by his hard reasoning power and by his devotion to fact? Here I am gravely retailing the gossip of a woman who tells me how her soul may be projected from her body, and how, while she lies in a lethargy, she can control the actions of people at a distance. Do I accept it? Certainly not. She must prove and re-prove before I yield a point. But if I am still a sceptic, I have at least ceased to be a scoffer. We are to have a sitting this evening, and she is to try if she can produce any mesmeric effect upon me. If she can, it will make an excellent starting point for our investigation. No one can accuse me, at any rate, of complicity. If she cannot, we must try and find some subject who will be like Caesar's wife. Wilson is perfectly impervious.

10 P. M. I believe that I am on the threshold of an epoch-making investigation. To have the power of examining these phenomena from inside to have an organism which will respond, and at the same time a brain which will appreciate and criticise that is surely a unique advantage. I am quite sure that Wilson would give five years of his life to be as susceptible as I have proved myself to be.

There was no one present except Wilson and his wife. I was seated with my head leaning back, and Miss Penclosa, standing in front and a little to the left, used the same long, sweeping strokes as with Agatha. At each of them a warm current of air seemed to strike me, and to suffuse a thrill and glow all through me from head to foot. My eyes were fixed upon Miss Penclosa's face, but as I gazed the features seemed to blur and to fade away. I was conscious only of her own eyes looking down at me, grey, deep, inscrutable. Larger they grew and larger, until they changed suddenly into two mountain lakes toward which I seemed to be falling with horrible rapidity. I shuddered, and as I did so some deeper stratum of thought told me that the shudder represented the rigour which I had observed in Agatha. An instant later I struck the surface of the lakes, now joined into one, and down I went beneath the water with a fulness in my head and a buzzing in my ears. Down I went, down, down, and then with a swoop up again until I could see the light streaming brightly through the green water. I was almost at the surface when the word

'Awake!' rang through my head, and, with a start, I found myself back in the armchair, with Miss Penclosa leaning on her crutch, and Wilson, his notebook in his hand, peeping over her shoulder. No heaviness or weariness was left behind. On the contrary, though it is only an hour or so since the experiment, I feel so wakeful that I am more inclined for my study than my bedroom. I see quite a vista of interesting experiments extending before us, and am all impatience to begin upon them.

March 27. A blank day, as Miss Penclosa goes with Wilson and his wife to the Suttons'. Have begun Binet and Ferre's 'Animal Magnetism.' What strange, deep waters these are!

Results, results, results and the cause an absolute mystery. It is stimulating to the imagination, but I must be on my guard against that. Let us have no inferences nor deductions, and nothing but solid facts. I KNOW that the mesmeric trance is true; I KNOW that mesmeric suggestion is true; I KNOW that I am myself sensitive to this force. That is my present position. I have a large new notebook which shall be devoted entirely to scientific detail.

Long talk with Agatha and Mrs Marden in the evening about our marriage. We think that the summer vac. (the beginning of it) would be the best time for the wedding. Why should we delay? I grudge even those few months. Still, as Mrs Marden says, there are a good many things to be arranged.

March 28. Mesmerized again by Miss Penclosa. Experience much the same as before, save that insensibility came on more quickly. See Notebook A for temperature of room, barometric pressure, pulse, and respiration as taken by Professor Wilson.

March 29. Mesmerized again. Details in Notebook A.

March 30. Sunday, and a blank day. I grudge any interruption of our experiments. At present they merely embrace the physical signs which go with slight, with complete, and with extreme insensibility. Afterwards we hope to pass on to the phenomena of suggestion and of lucidity. Professors have demonstrated these things upon women at Nancy and at the Salpetriere. It will be more convincing when a woman demonstrates it upon a professor, with a second professor as a witness. And that I should be the subject I, the sceptic, the materialist! At least, I have shown that my devotion to science is greater than to my own personal consistency. The eating of our own words is the greatest sacrifice which truth ever requires of us.

My neighbour, Charles Sadler, the handsome young demonstrator of anatomy, came in this evening to return a volume of Virchow's 'Archives' which I had lent him. I call him young, but, as a matter of fact, he is a year older than I am.

'I understand, Gilroy,' said he, 'that you are being experimented upon by Miss Penclosa.'

'Well,' he went on, when I had acknowledged it, 'if I were you, I should not let it go any further. You will think me very impertinent, no doubt, but, none the less, I feel it to be my duty to advise you to have no more to do with her.'

Of course I asked him why.

'I am so placed that I cannot enter into particulars as freely as I could wish,' said he.

'Miss Penclosa is the friend of my friend, and my position is a delicate one. I can only say this: that I have myself been the subject of some of the woman's experiments, and that they have left a most unpleasant impression upon my mind.'

He could hardly expect me to be satisfied with that, and I tried hard to get something more definite out of him, but without success. Is it conceivable that he could be jealous at my having superseded him? Or is he one of those men of science who feel personally injured when facts run counter to their preconceived opinions? He cannot seriously suppose that because he has some vague grievance I am, therefore, to abandon a series of experiments which promise to be so fruitful of results. He appeared to be annoyed at the light way in which I treated his shadowy warnings, and we parted with some little coldness on both sides.

March 31. Mesmerized by Miss P.

April 1. Mesmerized by Miss P. (Notebook A.)

April 2. Mesmerized by Miss P. (Sphygmographic chart taken by Professor Wilson.)

April 3. It is possible that this course of mesmerism may be a little trying to the general constitution. Agatha says that I am thinner and darker under the eyes. I am conscious of a nervous irritability which I had not observed in myself before. The least noise, for example, makes me start, and the stupidity of a student causes me exasperation instead of amusement. Agatha wishes me to stop, but I tell her that every course of study is trying, and that one can never attain a result without paying some price for it. When she sees the sensation which my forthcoming paper on 'The Relation between Mind and Matter' may make, she will understand that it is worth a little nervous wear and tear. I should not be surprised if I got my F. R. S. over it.

Mesmerized again in the evening. The effect is produced more rapidly now, and the subjective visions are less marked. I keep full notes of each sitting. Wilson is leaving for town for a week or ten days, but we shall not interrupt the experiments, which depend for their value as much upon my sensations as on his observations.

April 4. I must be carefully on my guard. A complication has crept into our experiments which I had not reckoned upon. In my eagerness for scientific facts I have been foolishly blind to the human relations between Miss Penclosa and myself. I can write here what I would not breathe to a living soul. The unhappy woman appears to have formed an attachment for me.

I should not say such a thing, even in the privacy of my own intimate journal, if it had not come to such a pass that it is impossible to ignore it. For some time, that is, for the last week, there have been signs which I have brushed aside and refused to think of. Her brightness when I come, her dejection when I go, her eagerness that I should come often, the expression of her eyes, the tone of her voice I tried to think that they meant nothing, and were, perhaps, only her ardent West Indian manner. But last night, as I awoke from the mesmeric sleep, I put out my hand, unconsciously, involuntarily, and clasped hers. When I came fully to myself, we were sitting with them locked, she looking up at me with an expectant smile. And the horrible thing was that I felt impelled to say what she expected me to say. What a false wretch I should have been! How I should have loathed myself today had I yielded to the temptation of that moment! But, thank God, I was strong enough to spring up and hurry from the room. I was rude, I fear, but I could not, no, I COULD not, trust myself another moment. I, a gentleman, a man of honour, engaged to one of the sweetest girls in England and yet in a moment of reasonless passion I nearly professed love for this woman whom I hardly know. She is far older than myself and a cripple. It is monstrous, odious; and yet the impulse was so strong that, had I stayed another minute in her presence, I should have committed myself. What was it? I have to teach others the workings of our organism, and what do I know of it myself? Was it the sudden upcropping of some lower stratum in my nature a brutal primitive instinct suddenly asserting itself? I could almost believe the tales of obsession by evil spirits, so overmastering was the feeling.

Well, the incident places me in a most unfortunate position. On the one hand, I am very loath to abandon a series of experiments which have already gone so far, and which promise such brilliant results. On the other, if this unhappy woman has conceived a passion for me. But surely even now I must have made some hideous mistake. She, with her age and her deformity! It is impossible. And then she knew about Agatha. She understood how I was placed. She only smiled out of amusement, perhaps, when in my dazed state I seized her hand. It was my half-mesmerized brain which gave it a meaning, and sprang with such bestial swiftness to meet it. I wish I could persuade myself that it was indeed so. On the whole, perhaps, my wisest plan would be to postpone our other experiments until Wilson's return. I have written a note to Miss Penclosa, therefore, making no allusion to last night, but saying that a press of work would cause me to interrupt our sittings for a few days. She has answered, formally enough, to say that if I should change my mind I should find her at home at the usual hour.

10 P. M. Well, well, what a thing of straw I am! I am coming to know myself better of late, and the more I know the lower I fall in my own estimation. Surely I was not always so weak as this. At four o'clock I should have smiled had anyone told me that I should go to Miss Penclosa's tonight, and yet, at eight, I was at Wilson's door as usual. I don't know how it occurred. The influence of habit, I suppose. Perhaps there is a mesmeric craze as there is an opium craze,

and I am a victim to it. I only know that as I worked in my study I became more and more uneasy. I fidgeted. I worried. I could not concentrate my mind upon the papers in front of me. And then, at last, almost before I knew what I was doing, I seized my hat and hurried round to keep my usual appointment.

We had an interesting evening. Mrs. Wilson was present during most of the time, which prevented the embarrassment which one at least of us must have felt. Miss Penclosa's manner was quite the same as usual, and she expressed no surprise at my having come in spite of my note. There was nothing in her bearing to show that yesterday's incident had made any impression upon her, and so I am inclined to hope that I overrated it.

April 6 (evening). No, no, no, I did not overrate it. I can no longer attempt to conceal from myself that this woman has conceived a passion for me. It is monstrous, but it is true. Again, tonight, I awoke from the mesmeric trance to find my hand in hers, and to suffer that odious feeling which urges me to throw away my honour, my career, everything, for the sake of this creature who, as I can plainly see when I am away from her influence, possesses no single charm upon earth. But when I am near her, I do not feel this. She rouses something in me, something evil, something I had rather not think of. She paralyzes my better nature, too, at the moment when she stimulates my worse. Decidedly it is not good for me to be near her.

Last night was worse than before. Instead of flying I actually sat for some time with my hand in hers talking over the most intimate subjects with her. We spoke of Agatha, among other things. What could I have been dreaming of? Miss Penclosa said that she was conventional, and I agreed with her. She spoke once or twice in a disparaging way of her, and I did not protest. What a creature I have been!

Weak as I have proved myself to be, I am still strong enough to bring this sort of thing to an end. It shall not happen again. I have sense enough to fly when I cannot fight. From this Sunday night onward I shall never sit with Miss Penclosa again. Never! Let the experiments go, let the research come to an end; anything is better than facing this monstrous temptation which drags me so low. I have said nothing to Miss Penclosa, but I shall simply stay away. She can tell the reason without any words of mine.

April 7. Have stayed away as I said. It is a pity to ruin such an interesting investigation, but it would be a greater pity still to ruin my life, and I KNOW that I cannot trust myself with that woman.

11 P. M. God help me! What is the matter with me? Am I going mad? Let me try and be calm and reason with myself. First of all I shall set down exactly what occurred.

It was nearly eight when I wrote the lines with which this day begins. Feeling strangely restless and uneasy, I left my rooms and walked round to spend the evening with Agatha and her mother. They both remarked that I was pale and haggard. About nine Professor Pratt-Haldane came in, and we played a game of whist. I tried hard to concentrate my attention upon the cards, but the feeling of restlessness grew and grew until I found it impossible to struggle against it. I simply COULD not sit still at the table. At last, in the very middle of a hand, I threw my cards down and, with some sort of an incoherent apology about having an appointment, I rushed from the room. As if in a dream I have a vague recollection of tearing through the hall, snatching my hat from the stand, and slamming the door behind me. As in a dream, too, I have the impression of the double line of gas lamps, and my bespattered boots tell me that I must have run down the middle of the road. It was all misty and strange and unnatural. I came to Wilson's house; I saw Mrs Wilson and I saw Miss Penclosa. I hardly recall what we talked about, but I do remember that Miss P. shook the head of her crutch at me in a playful way, and accused me of being late and of losing interest in our experiments. There was no mesmerism, but I stayed some time and have only just returned.

My brain is quite clear again now, and I can think over what has occurred. It is absurd to suppose that it is merely weakness and force of habit. I tried to explain it in that way the other night, but it will no longer suffice. It is something much deeper and more terrible than that. Why, when I was at the Mardens' whist table, I was dragged away as if the noose of a rope had been cast around me. I can no longer disguise it from myself. The woman has her grip upon me. I am in her clutch. But I must keep my head and reason it out and see what is best to be done.

But what a blind fool I have been! In my enthusiasm over my research I have walked straight into the pit, although it lay gaping before me. Did she not herself warn me? Did she not tell me, as I can read in my own journal, that when she has acquired power over a subject she can make him do her will? And she has acquired that power over me. I am for the moment at the beck and call of this creature with the crutch. I must come when she wills it. I must do as she wills. Worst of all, I must feel as she wills. I loathe her and fear her, yet, while I am under the spell, she can doubtless make me love her.

There is some consolation in the thought, then, that those odious impulses for which I have blamed myself do not really come from me at all. They are all transferred from her, little as I could have guessed it at the time. I feel cleaner and lighter for the thought.

April 8. Yes, now, in broad daylight, writing coolly and with time for reflection, I am compelled to confirm everything which I wrote in my journal last night. I am in a horrible position, but, above all, I must not lose my head. I must pit my intellect against her powers. After all, I am no silly puppet, to dance at the end of a string. I have energy, brains, courage. For all her devil's tricks I may beat her yet. May! I MUST, or what is to become of me?

Let me try to reason it out! This woman, by her own explanation, can dominate my nervous organism. She can project herself into my body and take command of it. She has a parasite soul; yes, she is a parasite, a monstrous parasite. She creeps into my frame as the hermit crab does into the whelk's shell. I am powerless What can I do? I am dealing with forces of which I know nothing. And I can tell no one of my trouble. They would set me down as a madman. Certainly, if it got noised abroad, the university would say that they had no need of a devil-ridden professor. And Agatha! No, no, I must face it alone.

Chapter III

I read over my notes of what the woman said when she spoke about her powers. There is one point which fills me with dismay. She implies that when the influence is slight the subject knows what he is doing, but cannot control himself, whereas when it is strongly exerted he is absolutely unconscious. Now, I have always known what I did, though less so last night than on the previous occasions. That seems to mean that she has never yet exerted her full powers upon me. Was ever a man so placed before?

Yes, perhaps there was, and very near me, too. Charles Sadler must know something of this! His vague words of warning take a meaning now. Oh, if I had only listened to him then, before I helped by these repeated sittings to forge the links of the chain which binds me! But I will see him today. I will apologize to him for having treated his warning so lightly. I will see if he can advise me.

4 P. M. No, he cannot. I have talked with him, and he showed such surprise at the first words in which I tried to express my unspeakable secret that I went no further. As far as I can gather (by hints and inferences rather than by any statement), his own experience was limited to some words or looks such as I have myself endured. His abandonment of Miss Penclosa is in itself a sign that he was never really in her toils. Oh, if he only knew his escape! He has to thank his phlegmatic Saxon temperament for it. I am black and Celtic, and this hag's clutch is deep in my nerves. Shall I ever get it

out? Shall I ever be the same man that I was just one short fortnight ago?

Let me consider what I had better do. I cannot leave the university in the middle of the term. If I were free, my course would be obvious. I should start at once and travel in Persia. But would she allow me to start? And could her influence not reach me in Persia, and bring me back to within touch of her crutch? I can only find out the limits of this hellish power by my own bitter experience. I will fight and fight and fight and what can I do more?

I know very well that about eight o'clock tonight that craving for her society, that irresistible restlessness, will come upon me. How shall I overcome it? What shall I do? I must make it impossible for me to leave the room. I shall lock the door and throw the key out of the window. But, then, what am I to do in the morning? Never mind about the morning. I must at all costs break this chain which holds me.

April 9. Victory! I have done splendidly! At seven o'clock last night I took a hasty dinner, and then locked myself up in my bedroom and dropped the key into the garden. I chose a cheery novel, and lay in bed for three hours trying to read it, but really in a horrible state of trepidation, expecting every instant that I should become conscious of the impulse. Nothing of the sort occurred, however, and I awoke this morning with the feeling that a black nightmare had been lifted off me. Perhaps the creature realized what I had done, and understood that it was useless to try to influence me. At any rate, I have beaten her once, and if I can do it once, I can do it again.

It was most awkward about the key in the morning. Luckily, there was an under-gardener below, and I asked him to throw it up. No doubt he thought I had just dropped it. I will have doors and windows screwed up and six stout men to hold me down in my bed before I will surrender myself to be hag-ridden in this way.

I had a note from Mrs Marden this afternoon asking me to go around and see her. I intended to do so in any case, but had not excepted to find bad news waiting for me. It seems that the Armstrongs, from whom Agatha has expectations, are due home from Adelaide in the Aurora, and that they have written to Mrs Marden and her to meet them in town. They will probably be away for a month or six weeks, and, as the Aurora is due on Wednesday, they must go at once tomorrow, if they are ready in time. My consolation is that when we meet again there will be no more parting between Agatha and me.

'I want you to do one thing, Agatha,' said I, when we were alone together. 'If you should happen to meet Miss Penclosa, either in town or here, you must promise me never again to allow her to mesmerize you.'

Agatha opened her eyes.

'Why, it was only the other day that you were saying how interesting it all was, and how determined you were to finish your experiments.'

'I know, but I have changed my mind since then.'

'And you won't have it anymore?'

'No.'

'I am so glad, Austin. You can't think how pale and worn you have been lately. It was really our principal objection to going to London now that we did not wish to leave you when you were so pulled down. And your manner has been so strange occasionally especially that night when you left poor Professor Pratt-Haldane to play dummy. I am convinced that these experiments are very bad for your nerves.'

'I think so, too, dear.'

'And for Miss Penclosa's nerves as well. You have heard that she is ill?'

'No.'

'Mrs Wilson told us so last night. She described it as a nervous fever. Professor Wilson is coming back this week, and of course Mrs Wilson is very anxious that Miss Penclosa should be well again then, for he has quite a programme of experiments which he is anxious to carry out.'

I was glad to have Agatha's promise, for it was enough that this woman should have one of us in her clutch. On the other hand, I was disturbed to hear about Miss Penclosa's illness. It rather discounts the victory which I appeared to win last night. I remember that she said that loss of health interfered with her power. That may be why I was able to hold my own so easily. Well, well, I must take the same precautions tonight and see what comes of it. I am childishly frightened when I think of her.

April 10. All went very well last night. I was amused at the gardener's face when I had again to hail him this morning and to ask him to throw up my key. I shall get a name among the servants if this sort of thing goes on. But the great point is that I stayed in my room without the slightest inclination to leave it. I do believe that I am shaking myself clear of this incredible bond or is it only that the woman's power is in abeyance until she recovers her strength? I can but pray for the best.

The Mardens left this morning, and the brightness seems to have gone out of the spring sunshine. And yet it is very beautiful also as it gleams on the green chestnuts opposite my windows, and gives a touch of gayety to the heavy, lichen-mottled walls of the old colleges. How sweet and gentle and soothing is Nature! Who would think that there lurked in her also such vile forces, such odious possibilities! For of course I understand that this dreadful thing which has sprung out at me is neither supernatural nor even preternatural. No, it is a natural force which this woman can use and society is ignorant of. The mere fact that it ebbs with her strength shows how entirely it is subject to physical laws. If I had time, I might probe it to the bottom and lay my hands upon its antidote. But you cannot tame the tiger when you are beneath his claws. You can but try to writhe away from him. Ah, when I look in the glass and see my own dark eyes and clear-cut Spanish face, I long for a vitriol splash or a bout of the smallpox. One or the other might have saved me from this calamity.

I am inclined to think that I may have trouble tonight. There are two things which make me fear so. One is that I met Mrs. Wilson in the street, and that she tells me that Miss Penclosa is better, though still weak. I find myself wishing in my heart that the illness had been her last. The other is that Professor Wilson comes back in a day or two, and his presence would act as a constraint upon her. I should not fear our interviews if a third person were present. For both these reasons I have a presentiment of trouble tonight, and I shall take the same precautions as before.

April 10. No, thank God, all went well last night. I really could not face the gardener again. I locked my door and thrust the key underneath it, so that I had to ask the maid to let me out in the morning. But the precaution was really not needed, for I never had any inclination to go out at all. Three evenings in succession at home! I am surely near the end of my troubles, for Wilson will be home again either today or tomorrow. Shall I tell him of what I have gone through or not? I am convinced that I should not have the slightest sympathy from him. He would look upon me as an interesting case, and read a paper about me at the next meeting of the Psychical Society, in which he would gravely discuss the possibility of my being a deliberate liar, and weigh it against the chances of my being in an early stage of lunacy. No, I shall get no comfort out of Wilson.

I am feeling wonderfully fit and well. I don't think I ever lectured with greater spirit. Oh, if I could only get this shadow off my life, how happy I should be! Young, fairly wealthy, in the front rank of my profession, engaged to a beautiful and charming girl have I not everything which a man could ask for? Only one thing to trouble me, but what a thing it is!

Midnight. I shall go mad. Yes, that will be the end of it. I shall go mad. I am not far from it now. My head throbs as I rest it on my hot hand. I am quivering all over like a scared horse. Oh, what a night I have had! And yet I have some cause to be satisfied also.

At the risk of becoming the laughingstock of my own servant, I again slipped my key under the door, imprisoning myself for the night. Then, finding it too early to go to bed, I lay down with my clothes on and began to read one of Dumas's novels. Suddenly I was gripped and dragged from the couch. It is only thus that I can describe the overpowering nature of the force which pounced upon me. I clawed at the coverlet. I clung to the woodwork. I believe that I screamed out in my frenzy. It was all useless, hopeless. I MUST go. There was no way out of it. It was only at the outset that I resisted. The force soon became too overmastering for that. I thank goodness that there were no watchers there to interfere with me. I could not have answered for myself if there had been. And, besides the determination to get out, there came to me, also, the keenest and coolest judgment in choosing my means. I lit a candle and endeavoured, kneeling in front of the door, to pull the key through with the feather end of a quill pen. It was just too short and pushed it further away. Then with quiet persistence I got a paper knife out of one of the drawers, and with that I managed to draw the key back. I opened the door, stepped into my study, took a photograph of myself from the bureau, wrote something across it, placed it in the inside pocket of my coat, and then started off for Wilson's.

It was all wonderfully clear, and yet disassociated from the rest of my life, as the incidents of even the most vivid dream might be. A peculiar double consciousness possessed me. There was the predominant alien will, which was bent upon drawing me to the side of its owner, and there was the feebler protesting personality, which I recognized as being myself, tugging feebly at the overmastering impulse as a led terrier might at its chain. I can remember recognizing these two conflicting forces, but I recall nothing of my walk, nor of how I was admitted to the house.

Very vivid, however, is my recollection of how I met Miss Penclosa. She was reclining on the sofa in the little boudoir in which our experiments had usually been carried out. Her head was rested on her hand, and a tiger-skin rug had been partly drawn over her. She looked up expectantly as I entered, and, as the lamp light fell upon her face, I could see that she was very pale and thin, with dark hollows under her eyes. She smiled at me, and pointed to a stool beside her. It was with her left hand that she pointed, and I, running eagerly forward, seized it, I loathe myself as I think of it, and pressed it passionately to my lips. Then, seating myself upon the stool, and still retaining her hand, I gave her the photograph which I had brought with me, and talked and talked and talked of my love for her, of my grief over her illness, of my joy at her recovery, of the misery it was to me to be absent a single evening from her side. She lay quietly looking down at me with imperious eyes and her provocative smile. Once I remember that she passed her hand over my hair as one caresses a dog; and it gave me pleasure the caress. I thrilled under it. I was her slave, body and soul, and for the moment I rejoiced in my slavery.

And then came the blessed change. Never tell me that there is not a Providence! I was on the brink of perdition. My feet were on the edge. Was it a coincidence that at that very instant help should come? No, no, no; there is a Providence, and its hand has drawn me back. There is something in the universe stronger than this devil woman with her tricks. Ah, what a balm to my heart it is to think so!

As I looked up at her I was conscious of a change in her. Her face, which had been pale before, was now ghastly. Her eyes were dull, and the lids drooped heavily over them. Above all, the look of serene confidence had gone from her features. Her mouth had weakened. Her forehead had puckered. She was frightened and undecided. And as I watched the change my own spirit fluttered and struggled, trying hard to tear itself from the grip which held it a grip which, from moment to moment, grew less secure.

'Austin,' she whispered, 'I have tried to do too much. I was not strong enough. I have not recovered yet from my illness. But I could not live longer without seeing you. You won't leave me, Austin? This is only a passing weakness. If you will only give me five minutes, I shall be myself again. Give me the small decanter from the table in the window.'

But I had regained my soul. With her waning strength the influence had cleared away from me and left me free. And I was aggressive bitterly, fiercely aggressive. For once at least I could make this woman understand what my real feelings toward her were. My soul was filled with a hatred as bestial as the love against which it was a reaction. It was the savage, murderous passion of the revolted serf. I could have taken the crutch from her side and beaten her face in with it. She threw her hands up, as if to avoid a blow, and cowered away from me into the corner of the settee.

'The brandy!' she gasped. 'The brandy!'

I took the decanter and poured it over the roots of a palm in the window. Then I snatched the photograph from her hand and tore it into a hundred pieces.

'You vile woman,' I said, 'if I did my duty to society, you would never leave this room alive!'

'I love you, Austin; I love you!' she wailed.

'Yes,' I cried, 'and Charles Sadler before. And how many others before that?'

'Charles Sadler!' she gasped. 'He has spoken to you? So, Charles Sadler, Charles Sadler!'

Her voice came through her white lips like a snake's hiss.

'Yes, I know you, and others shall know you, too. You shameless creature! You knew how I stood. And yet you used your vile power to bring me to your side. You may, perhaps, do so again, but at least you will remember that you have heard me say that I love Miss Marden from the bottom of my soul, and that I loathe you, abhor you!

'The very sight of you and the sound of your voice fill me with horror and disgust. The thought of you is repulsive. That is how I feel toward you, and if it pleases you by your tricks to draw me again to your side as you have done tonight, you will at least, I should think, have little satisfaction in trying to make a lover out of a man who has told you his real opinion of you. You may put what words you will into my mouth, but you cannot help remembering.'

I stopped, for the woman's head had fallen back, and she had fainted. She could not bear to hear what I had to say to her! What a glow of satisfaction it gives me to think that, come what may, in the future she can never misunderstand my true feelings toward her. But what will occur in the future? What will she do next? I dare not think of it. Oh, if only I could hope that she will leave me alone! But when I think of what I said to her. Never mind; I have been stronger than she for once.

April 11. I hardly slept last night, and found myself in the morning so unstrung and feverish that I was compelled to ask Pratt-Haldane to do my lecture for me. It is the first that I have ever missed. I rose at midday, but my head is aching, my hands quivering, and my nerves in a pitiable state.

Who should come round this evening but Wilson. He has just come back from London, where he has lectured, read papers, convened meetings, exposed a medium, conducted a series of experiments on thought transference, entertained Professor Richet of Paris, spent hours gazing into a crystal, and obtained some evidence as to the passage of matter through matter. All this he poured into my ears in a single gust.

'But you!' he cried at last. 'You are not looking well. And Miss Penclosa is quite prostrated today. How about the experiments?'

'I have abandoned them.'

'Tut, tut! Why?'

'The subject seems to me to be a dangerous one.'

Out came his big brown notebook.

'This is of great interest,' said he. 'What are your grounds for saying that it is a dangerous one? Please give your facts in chronological order, with approximate dates and names of reliable witnesses with their permanent addresses.'

'First of all,' I asked, 'would you tell me whether you have collected any cases where the mesmerist has gained a command over the subject and has used it for evil purposes?'

'Dozens!' he cried exultantly. 'Crime by suggestion.'

'I don't mean suggestion. I mean where a sudden impulse comes from a person at a distance an uncontrollable impulse.'

'Obsession!' he shrieked, in an ecstasy of delight. 'It is the rarest condition. We have eight cases, five well-attested. You don't mean to say.'

His exultation made him hardly articulate.

'No, I don't,' said I. 'Good evening! You will excuse me, but I am not very well tonight.'

And so at last I got rid of him, still brandishing his pencil and his notebook. My troubles may be bad to hear, but at least it is better to hug them to myself than to have myself exhibited by Wilson, like a freak at a fair. He has lost sight of human beings. Everything to him is a case and a phenomenon. I will die before I speak to him again upon the matter.

April 12. Yesterday was a blessed day of quiet, and I enjoyed an uneventful night. Wilson's presence is a great consolation. What can the woman do now? Surely, when she has heard me say what I have said, she will conceive the same disgust for me which I have for her. She could not, no, she COULD not, desire to have a lover who had insulted her so.

No, I believe I am free from her love but how about her hate? Might she not use these powers of hers for revenge? Tut! Why should I frighten myself over shadows? She will forget about me, and I shall forget about her, and all will be well.

April 13. My nerves have quite recovered their tone. I really believe that I have conquered the creature. But I must confess to living in some suspense. She is well again, for I hear that she was driving with Mrs Wilson in the High Street in the afternoon.

April 14. I do wish I could get away from the place altogether. I shall fly to Agatha's side the very day that the term closes. I suppose it is pitiably weak of me, but this woman gets upon my nerves most terribly. I have seen her again, and I have spoken with her.

It was just after lunch, and I was smoking a cigarette in my study, when I heard the step of my servant Murray in the passage. I was languidly conscious that a second step was audible behind, and had hardly troubled myself to speculate who it might be, when suddenly a slight noise brought me out of my chair with my skin creeping with apprehension. I had never particularly observed before what sort of sound the tapping of a crutch was, but my quivering nerves told me that I heard it now in the sharp wooden clack which alternated with the muffled thud of the footfall. Another instant and my servant had shown her in.

I did not attempt the usual conventions of society, nor did she. I simply stood with the smouldering cigarette in my hand, and gazed at her. She in her turn looked silently at me, and at her look I remembered how in these very pages I had tried to define the expression of her eyes, whether they were furtive or fierce. Today they were fierce coldly and inexorably so.

'Well,' said she at last, 'are you still of the same mind as when I saw you last?'

'I have always been of the same mind.'

'Let us understand each other, Professor Gilroy,' said she slowly. 'I am not a very safe person to trifle with, as you should realize by now. It was you who asked me to enter into a series of experiments with you, it was you who won my affections, it was you who professed your love for me, it was you who brought me your own photograph with words of affection upon it, and, finally, it was you who on the very same evening thought fit to insult me most outrageously, addressing me as no man has ever dared to speak to me yet. Tell me that those words came from you in a moment of passion and I am prepared to forget and to forgive them. You did not mean what you said, Austin? You do not really hate me?'

I might have pitied this deformed woman such a longing for love broke suddenly through the menace of her eyes. But then I thought of what I had gone through, and my heart set like flint.

'If ever you heard me speak of love,' said I, 'you know very well that it was your voice which spoke, and not mine. The only words of truth which I have ever been able to say to you are those which you heard when last we met.'

'I know. Someone has set you against me. It was he!'

She tapped with her crutch upon the floor.

'Well, you know very well that I could bring you this instant crouching like a spaniel to my feet. You will not find me again in my hour of weakness, when you can insult me with impunity. Have a care what you are doing, Professor Gilroy. You stand in a terrible position. You have not yet realized the hold which I have upon you.'

I shrugged my shoulders and turned away.

'Well,' said she, after a pause, 'if you despise my love, I must see what can be done with fear. You smile, but the day will come when you will come screaming to me for pardon. Yes, you will grovel on the ground before me, proud as you are, and you will curse the day that ever you turned me from your best friend into your most bitter enemy. Have a care, Professor Gilroy!'

I saw a white hand shaking in the air, and a face which was scarcely human, so convulsed was it with passion. An instant later she was gone, and I heard the quick hobble and tap receding down the passage.

But she has left a weight upon my heart. Vague presentiments of coming misfortune lie heavy upon me. I try in vain to persuade myself that these are only words of empty anger. I can remember those relentless eyes too clearly to think so. What shall I do ah, what shall I do? I am no longer master of my own soul. At any moment this loathsome parasite may creep into me, and then I must tell someone my hideous secret I must tell it or go mad. If I had someone to sympathize and advise! Wilson is out of the question. Charles Sadler would understand me only so far as his own experience carries him. Pratt-Haldane! He is a well-balanced man, a man of great common sense and resource. I will go to him. I will tell him everything. God grant that he may be able to advise me!

Chapter IV

6.45 P. M. No, it is useless. There is no human help for me; I must fight this out single-handed. Two courses lie before me. I might become this woman's lover. Or I must endure such persecutions as she can inflict upon me. Even if none come, I shall live in a hell of apprehension. But she may torture me, she may drive me mad, she may kill me: I will never, never, never give in. What can she inflict which would be worse than the loss of Agatha, and the knowledge that I am a perjured liar, and have forfeited the name of gentleman?

Pratt-Haldane was most amiable, and listened with all politeness to my story. But when I looked at his heavy-set features, his slow eyes, and the ponderous study furniture which surrounded him, I could hardly tell him what I had come to say. It was all so substantial, so material. And, besides, what would I myself have said a short month ago if one of my colleagues had come to me with a story of demonic possession? Perhaps. I should have been less patient than he was. As it was, he took notes of my statement, asked me how much tea I drank, how many hours I slept, whether I had been overworking much, had I had sudden pains in the head, evil dreams, singing in the ears, flashes before the eyes all questions which pointed to his belief that brain congestion was at the bottom of my trouble. Finally he dismissed me with a great many platitudes about open-air exercise, and avoidance of nervous excitement. His prescription, which was for chloral and bromide, I rolled up and threw into the gutter.

No, I can look for no help from any human being. If I consult any more, they may put their heads together and I may find myself in an asylum. I can but grip my courage with both hands, and pray that an honest man may not be abandoned.

April 10. It is the sweetest spring within the memory of man. So green, so mild, so beautiful! Ah, what a contrast between nature without and my own soul so torn with doubt and terror! It has been an uneventful day, but I know that I am on the edge of an abyss. I know it, and yet I go on with the routine of my life. The one bright spot is that Agatha is happy and well and out of all danger. If this creature had a hand on each of us, what might she not do?

April 16. The woman is ingenious in her torments. She knows how fond I am of my work, and how highly my lectures are thought of. So it is from that point that she now attacks me. It will end, I can see, in my losing my professorship, but I will fight to the finish. She shall not drive me out of it without a struggle.

I was not conscious of any change during my lecture this morning save that for a minute or two I had a dizziness and swimminess which rapidly passed away. On the contrary, I congratulated myself upon having made my subject (the functions of the red corpuscles) both interesting and clear. I was surprised, therefore, when a student came into my laboratory immediately after the lecture, and complained of being puzzled by the discrepancy between my statements and those in the textbooks. He showed me his notebook, in which I was reported as having in one portion of the lecture championed the most outrageous and unscientific heresies. Of course I denied it, and declared that he had misunderstood me, but on comparing his notes with those of his companions, it became clear that he was right, and that I really had made some most preposterous statements. Of course I shall explain it away as being the result of a moment of aberration, but I feel only too sure that it will be the first of a series. It is but a month now to the end of the session, and I pray that I may be able to hold out until then.

April 26. Ten days have elapsed since I have had the heart to make any entry in my journal. Why should I record my own humiliation and degradation? I had vowed never to open it again. And yet the force of habit is strong, and here I find myself taking up once more the record of my own dreadful experiences in much the same spirit in which a suicide has been known to take notes of the effects of the poison which killed him.

Well, the crash which I had foreseen has come and that no further back than yesterday. The university authorities have taken my lectureship from me. It has been done in the most delicate way, purporting to be a temporary measure to relieve me from the effects of overwork, and to give me the opportunity of recovering my health. Nonetheless, it has been done, and I am no longer Professor Gilroy. The laboratory is still in my charge, but I have little doubt that that also will soon go.

The fact is that my lectures had become the laughingstock of the university. My class was crowded with students who came to see and hear what the eccentric professor would do or say next. I cannot go into the detail of my humiliation. Oh, that devilish woman! There is no depth of buffoonery and imbecility to which she has not forced me. I would begin my lecture clearly and well, but always with the sense of a coming eclipse. Then as I felt the influence I would struggle against it, striving with clenched hands and beads of sweat upon my brow to get the better of it, while the students, hearing my incoherent words and watching my contortions, would roar with laughter at the antics of their professor. And then, when she had once fairly mastered me, out would come the most outrageous things silly jokes, sentiments as though I were proposing a toast, snatches of ballads, personal abuse even against some member of my class. And then in a moment my brain would clear again, and my lecture would proceed decorously to the end. No wonder that my conduct has been the talk of the colleges. No wonder that the University Senate has been compelled to take official notice of such a scandal. Oh, that devilish woman!

And the most dreadful part of it all is my own loneliness. Here I sit in a commonplace English bow window, looking out upon a commonplace English street with its garish 'buses and its lounging policeman, and behind me there hangs a shadow which is out of all keeping with the age and place. In the home of knowledge I am weighed down and tortured by a power of which science knows nothing. No magistrate would listen to me. No paper would discuss my case. No doctor would believe my symptoms. My own most intimate friends would only look upon it as a sign of brain derangement. I am out of all touch with my kind. Oh, that devilish woman! Let her have a care! She may push me too far. When the law cannot help a man, he may make a law for himself.

She met me in the High Street yesterday evening and spoke to me. It was as well for her, perhaps, that it was not between the hedges of a lonely country road. She asked me with her cold smile whether I had been chastened yet. I did not deign to answer her.

'We must try another turn of the screw;' said she.

Have a care, my lady, have a care! I had her at my mercy once. Perhaps another chance may come.

April 28. The suspension of my lectureship has had the effect also of taking away her means of annoying me, and so I have enjoyed two blessed days of peace. After all, there is no reason to despair. Sympathy pours into me from all sides, and everyone agrees that it is my devotion to science and the arduous nature of my researches which have shaken my nervous system. I have had the kindest message from the council advising me to travel abroad, and expressing the confident hope that I may be able to resume all my duties by the beginning of the summer term. Nothing could be more flattering than their allusions to my career and to my services to the university. It is only in misfortune that one can test one's own popularity. This creature may weary of tormenting me, and then all may yet be well. May God grant it!

April 29. Our sleepy little town has had a small sensation. The only knowledge of crime which we ever have is when a rowdy undergraduate breaks a few lamps or comes to blows with a policeman. Last night, however, there was an attempt made to break into the branch of the Bank of England, and we are all in a flutter in consequence.

Parkenson, the manager, is an intimate friend of mine, and I found him very much excited when I walked round there after breakfast. Had the thieves broken into the counting-house, they would still have had the safes to reckon with, so that the defence was considerably stronger than the attack. Indeed, the latter does not appear to have ever been very formidable. Two of the lower windows have marks as if a chisel or some such instrument had been pushed under them to force them open. The police should have a good clue, for the woodwork had been done with green paint only the day before, and from the smears it is evident that some of it has found its way onto the criminal's hands or clothes.

4.30 P. M. Ah, that accursed woman! That thrice accursed woman! Never mind! She shall not beat me! No, she shall not! But, oh, the she-devil! She has taken my professorship. Now she would take my honour. Is there nothing I can do against her, nothing save – Ah, but, hard pushed as I am, I cannot bring myself to think of that!

It was about an hour ago that I went into my bedroom, and was brushing my hair before the glass, when suddenly my eyes lit upon something which left me so sick and cold that I sat down upon the edge of the bed and began to cry. It is many a long year since I shed tears, but all my nerve was gone, and I could but sob and sob in impotent grief and anger. There was my house jacket, the coat I usually wear after dinner, hanging on its peg by the wardrobe, with the right sleeve thickly crusted from wrist to elbow with daubs of green paint.

So this was what she meant by another turn of the screw! She had made a public imbecile of me. Now she would brand me as a criminal. This time she has failed. But how about the next? I dare not think of it and of Agatha and my poor old mother! I wish that I were dead!

Yes, this is the other turn of the screw. And this is also what she meant, no doubt, when she said that I had not realized yet the power she has over me. I look back at my account of my conversation with her, and I see how she declared that with a slight exertion of her will her subject would be conscious, and with a stronger one unconscious. Last night I was unconscious. I could have sworn that I slept soundly in my bed without so much as a dream. And yet those stains tell me that I dressed, made my way out, attempted to open the bank windows, and returned. Was I observed? Is it possible that someone saw me do it and followed me home? Ah, what a hell my life has become! I have no peace, no rest. But my patience is nearing its end.

10 P. M. I have cleaned my coat with turpentine. I do not think that anyone could have seen me. It was with my screwdriver that I made the marks. I found it all crusted with paint, and I have cleaned it. My head aches as if it would burst, and I have taken five grains of antipyrine. If it were not for Agatha, I should have taken fifty and had an end of it.

May 3. Three quiet days. This hell fiend is like a cat with a mouse. She lets me loose only to pounce upon me again. I am never so frightened as when everything is still. My physical state is deplorable, perpetual hiccough and ptosis of the left eyelid.

I have heard from the Mardens that they will be back the day after tomorrow. I do not know whether I am glad or sorry. They were safe in London. Once here they may be drawn into the miserable network in which I am myself struggling. And I must tell them of it. I cannot marry Agatha so long as I know that I am not responsible for my own actions. Yes, I must tell them, even if it brings everything to an end between us.

Tonight is the university ball, and I must go. God knows I never felt less in the humour for festivity, but I must not have it said that I am unfit to appear in public. If I am seen there, and have speech with some of the elders of the university it will go a long way toward showing them that it would be unjust to take my chair away from me.

10 P. M. I have been to the ball. Charles Sadler and I went together, but I have come away before him. I shall wait up for him, however, for, indeed, I fear to go to sleep these nights. He is a cheery, practical fellow, and a chat with him will steady my nerves. On the whole, the evening was a great success. I talked to everyone who has influence, and I think that I made them realize that my chair is not vacant quite yet. The creature was at the ball unable to dance, of course, but sitting with Mrs Wilson. Again and again her eyes rested upon me. They were almost the last things I saw before I left the room. Once, as I sat sideways to her, I watched her, and saw that her gaze was following someone else. It was Sadler, who was dancing at the time with the second Miss Thurston. To judge by her expression, it is well for him that he is not in her grip as I am. He does not know the escape he

has had. I think I hear his step in the street now, and I will go down and let him in. If he will.

May 4. Why did I break off in this way last night? I never went downstairs, after all at least, I have no recollection of doing so. But, on the other hand, I cannot remember going to bed. One of my hands is greatly swollen this morning, and yet I have no remembrance of injuring it yesterday. Otherwise, I am feeling all the better for last night's festivity. But I cannot understand how it is that I did not meet Charles Sadler when I so fully intended to do so. Is it possible – My God, it is only too probable! Has she been leading me some devil's dance again? I will go down to Sadler and ask him.

Midday. The thing has come to a crisis. My life is not worth living. But, if I am to die, then she shall come also. I will not leave her behind, to drive some other man mad as she has me. No, I have come to the limit of my endurance. She has made me as desperate and dangerous a man as walks the earth. God knows I have never had the heart to hurt a fly, and yet, if I had my hands now upon that woman, she should never leave this room alive. I shall see her this very day, and she shall learn what she has to expect from me.

I went to Sadler and found him, to my surprise, in bed. As I entered he sat up and turned a face toward me which sickened me as I looked at it.

'Why, Sadler, what has happened?' I cried, but my heart turned cold as I said it.

'Gilroy,' he answered, mumbling with his swollen lips, 'I have for some weeks been under the impression that you are a madman. Now I know it, and that you are a dangerous one as well. If it were not that I am unwilling to make a scandal in the college, you would now be in the hands of the police.'

'Do you mean,' I cried.

'I mean that as I opened the door last night you rushed out upon me, struck me with both your fists in the face, knocked me down, kicked me furiously in the side, and left me lying almost unconscious in the street. Look at your own hand bearing witness against you.'

Yes, there it was, puffed up, with sponge-like knuckles, as after some terrific blow. What could I do? Though he put me down as a madman, I must tell him all. I sat by his bed and went over all my troubles from the beginning. I poured them out with quivering hands and burning words which might have carried conviction to the most sceptical.

'She hates you and she hates me!' I cried. 'She revenged herself last night on both of us at once. She saw me leave the ball, and she must have seen you also. She knew how long it would take you to reach home. Then she had but to use her wicked will. Ah, your bruised face is a small thing beside my bruised soul!'

He was struck by my story. That was evident.

'Yes, yes, she watched me out of the room,' he muttered. 'She is capable of it. But is it possible that she has really reduced you to this? What do you intend to do?'

'To stop it!' I cried.

'I am perfectly desperate; I shall give her fair warning today, and the next time will be the last.'

'Do nothing rash,' said he.

'Rash!' I cried. 'The only rash thing is that I should postpone it another hour.'

With that I rushed to my room, and here I am on the eve of what may be the great crisis of my life. I shall start at once. I have gained one thing today, for I have made one man, at least, realize the truth of this monstrous experience of mine. And, if the worst should happen, this diary remains as a proof of the goad that has driven me.

Evening. When I came to Wilson's, I was shown up, and found that he was sitting with Miss Penclosa. For half an hour I had to endure his fussy talk about his recent research into the exact nature of the spiritualistic rap, while the creature and I sat in silence looking across the room at each other. I read a sinister amusement in her eyes, and she must have seen hatred and menace in mine. I had almost despaired of having speech with her when he was called from the room, and we were left for a few moments together.

'Well, Professor Gilroy or is it Mr Gilroy?' said she, with that bitter smile of hers. 'How is your friend Mr Charles Sadler after the ball?'

'You fiend!' I cried. 'You have come to the end of your tricks now. I will have no more of them. Listen to what I say.'

I strode across and shook her roughly by the shoulder.

'As sure as there is a God in heaven, I swear that if you try another of your deviltries upon me I will have your life for it. Come what may, I will have your life. I have come to the end of what a man can endure.'

'Accounts are not quite settled between us,' said she, with a passion that equalled my own. 'I can love, and I can hate. You had your choice. You chose to spurn the first; now you must test the other. It will take a little more to break your spirit, I see, but broken it shall be. Miss Marden comes back tomorrow, as I understand.'

'What has that to do with you?' I cried. 'It is a pollution that you should dare even to think of her. If I thought that you would harm her.'

She was frightened, I could see, though she tried to brazen it out. She read the black thought in my mind, and cowered away from me.

'She is fortunate in having such a champion,' said she. 'He actually dares to threaten a lonely woman. I must really congratulate Miss Marden upon her protector.'

The words were bitter, but the voice and manner were more acid still.

'There is no use talking,' said I. 'I only came here to tell you, and to tell you most solemnly, that your next outrage upon me will be your last.'

With that, as I heard Wilson's step upon the stair, I walked from the room. Ay, she may look venomous and deadly, but, for all that, she is beginning to see now that she has as much to fear from me as I can have from her. Murder! It has an ugly sound. But you don't talk of murdering a snake or of murdering a tiger. Let her have a care now.

May 5. I met Agatha and her mother at the station at eleven o'clock. She is looking so bright, so happy, so beautiful. And she was so overjoyed to see me. What have I done to deserve such love? I went back home with them, and we lunched together. All the troubles seem in a moment to have been shredded back from my life. She tells me that I am looking pale and worried and ill. The dear child puts it down to my loneliness and the perfunctory attentions of a housekeeper. I pray that she may never know the truth! May the shadow, if shadow there must be, lie ever black across my life and leave hers in the sunshine. I have just come back from them, feeling a new man. With her by my side I think that I could show a bold face to anything which life might send.

5 P. M. Now, let me try to be accurate. Let me try to say exactly how it occurred. It is fresh in my mind, and I can set it down correctly, though it is not likely that the time will ever come when I shall forget the doings of today.

I had returned from the Mardens' after lunch, and was cutting some microscopic sections in my freezing microtome, when in an instant I lost consciousness in the sudden hateful fashion which has become only too familiar to me of late.

When my senses came back to me I was sitting in a small chamber, very different from the one in which I had been working. It was cosy and bright, with chintz-covered settees, coloured hangings, and a thousand pretty little trifles upon the wall. A small ornamental clock ticked in front of me, and the hands pointed to half-past three. It was all quite familiar to me, and yet I stared about for a moment in a half-dazed way until my eyes fell upon a cabinet photograph of myself upon the top of the piano. On the other side stood one of Mrs Marden. Then, of course, I remembered where I was. It was Agatha's boudoir.

But how came I there, and what did I want? A horrible sinking came to my heart. Had I been sent here on some devilish errand? Had that errand already been done? Surely it must; otherwise, why should I be allowed to come back to consciousness? Oh, the agony of that moment! What had I done? I sprang to my feet in my despair, and as I did so a small glass bottle fell from my knees onto the carpet.

It was unbroken, and I picked it up. Outside was written 'Sulphuric Acid. Fort.' When I drew the round glass stopper, a thick fume rose slowly up, and a pungent, choking smell pervaded the room. I recognized it as one which I kept for chemical testing in my chambers. But why had I brought a bottle of vitriol into Agatha's chamber? Was it not this thick, reeking liquid with which jealous women had been known to mar the beauty of their rivals? My heart stood still as I held the bottle to the light. Thank God, it was full! No mischief had been done as yet. But had Agatha come in a minute sooner, was it not certain that the hellish parasite within me would have dashed the stuff into her. Ah, it will not bear to be thought of! But it must have been for that. Why else should I have brought it? At the thought of what I might have done my worn nerves broke down, and I sat shivering and twitching, the pitiable wreck of a man.

It was the sound of Agatha's voice and the rustle of her dress which restored me. I looked up, and saw her blue eyes, so full of tenderness and pity, gazing down at me.

'We must take you away to the country, Austin,' she said. 'You want rest and quiet. You look wretchedly ill.'

'Oh, it is nothing!' said I, trying to smile. 'It was only a momentary weakness. I am all right again now.'

'I am so sorry to keep you waiting. Poor boy, you must have been here quite half an hour! The vicar was in the drawing room, and, as I knew that you did not care for him,

I thought it better that Jane should show you up here. I thought the man would never go!'

'Thank God he stayed! Thank God he stayed!' I cried hysterically.

'Why, what is the matter with you, Austin?' she asked, holding my arm as I staggered up from the chair.

'Why are you glad that the vicar stayed? And what is this little bottle in your hand?'

'Nothing,' I cried, thrusting it into my pocket. 'But I must go. I have something important to do.'

'How stern you look, Austin! I have never seen your face like that. You are angry?'

'Yes, I am angry.'

'But not with me?'

'No, no, my darling! You would not understand.'

'But you have not told me why you came.'

'I came to ask you whether you would always love me no matter what I did, or what shadow might fall on my name. Would you believe in me and trust me however black appearances might be against me?'

'You know that I would, Austin.'

'Yes, I know that you would. What I do I shall do for you. I am driven to it. There is no other way out, my darling!'

I kissed her and rushed from the room.

The time for indecision was at an end. As long as the creature threatened my own prospects and my honour there might be a question as to what I should do. But now, when Agatha my innocent Agatha was endangered, my duty lay before me like a turnpike road. I had no weapon, but I never paused for that. What weapon should I need, when I felt

141

every muscle quivering with the strength of a frenzied man? I ran through the streets, so set upon what I had to do that I was only dimly conscious of the faces of friends whom I met dimly conscious also that Professor Wilson met me, running with equal precipitance in the opposite direction. Breathless but resolute I reached the house and rang the bell. A white-cheeked maid opened the door, and turned whiter yet when she saw the face that looked in at her.

'Show me up at once to Miss Penclosa,' I demanded.

'Sir,' she gasped, 'Miss Penclosa died this afternoon at half-past three!'

Finis

Workbooks From The Scheherazade Foundation

We hope that you have enjoyed this collection of stories, gleaned from varying cultural corners of the world, and that you have been entertained by them.

But, have you considered the deeper meanings and interwoven layers that lie hidden beneath the surface?

At The Scheherazade Foundation, we believe that Teaching-Stories contain wisdom, information, and marvels that have the power to transform the way we think, and thereby change our lives.

Employed as a bedrock of culture throughout the centuries – challenging established patterns of thinking, while passing on knowledge and values – tales such as the ones contained in this volume are a rich resource ready and waiting to be mined.

As an aid to help in the perception of less-obvious facets and layers, we have created a series of original Workbooks. Aimed at stimulating thought-provoking discussions and igniting deep reflection, these tools will assist in unlocking the power of Teaching-Stories.